There was something about the older sister that intrigued him.

Josh eyed her carefully. Wide dark brown eyes and dusky skin, a full mouth and a proud Roman nose that was somehow more enchanting than any upturned pug or cute button could ever be. His gaze traveled lower. Her long-sleeved tee didn't disguise a rounded chest, neither too large nor too small but just about right for cupping in his hands, and a long waist that tapered to hips his fingers itched to span. And those legs, stretched out in front of her…

He'd already felt how those legs felt wrapped around him, her lower half molding to his as they moved. He'd had people—other women— on his back before, but they had never been a stranger. Never a stranger with eyes that heated his imagination as much as his body.

"I don't suppose you're a virgin?" he asked suddenly.

Books by Anna Leonard

Silhouette Nocturne

The Night Serpent #48
The Hunted #86

Harlequin Nocturne

Shifter's Destiny #144

ANNA LEONARD

is the nom d'paranormal for fantasy/horror writer Laura Anne Gilman, who grew up wondering why none of the characters in her favorite Gothic novels ever seemed to know a damn thing about ghosts, vampires or how to run in high heels. She is delighted that the newest generation of heroines has a much better grasp on things. "Anna" lives in New York City, where either nothing or everything is paranormal....

Both can be reached via www.sff.net/people/lauraanne.gilman or http://cosanostradamus.blogspot.com.

SHIFTER'S DESTINY

ANNA LEONARD

HARLEQUIN®
entertain, enrich, inspire™

Recycling programs
for this product may
not exist in your area.

ISBN-13: 978-0-373-88554-1

SHIFTER'S DESTINY

www.Harlequin.com

Printed in U.S.A.

Dear Reader,

"Write something with weres!" my editor said, staring at me intently.*

"Werewolves have been done really well. So've werecats. And I know someone who wrote a were-guppy story. What's left?"

"You'll think of something. Guppies aren't sexy. What's sexy?"

Horses. Horses, as every girl knows, are sexy. They're freedom. Power. Independence. And, as every rider knows—stubborn as their cousin the mule.

And just like that, the mustang was born: fierce, independent, magical…proper cousins to their namesakes, the wild horses of America.

And, I discovered, a proper hero for a girl who needs help.

So if you've ever watched a herd of horses thundering across a field, ever grabbed a handful of mane or the leather of reins…or just wished hard that you could… this book's for you.

Enjoy!

Anna Leonard

*all right, the conversation didn't happen exactly that way. But almost.

For B. True friend, and hero-on-call.

Prologue

The smell of salt in the air normally invigorated him, made him willing to crawl out of the warm bed and see what the day would bring. But that morning he woke wishing instead for the sweeter smells of fresh grass and warm horseflesh, the sound of female voices and clattering hooves, instead of male shouts and the thump of a winch rising and lowering as the catch was brought in.

The wish settled deep inside him and became an itch, a dissatisfaction he couldn't quite identify.

It's time.

Josh groaned, and rolled over to shove his face into the pillow. No, he was going to sleep a little while longer. Long day ahead, and he needed a few more minutes of sleep.

It's time, the voice sounded again, and he realized, with a jolt, that the voice wasn't telling him to get up.

It was telling him to go home.

Chapter 1

The sun was high overhead, and the Saturday flea market was in full swing.

"You like? It's twenty dollars, but for you, sweetie, eighteen. No? All right, fifteen!" The vendor held up the brightly patterned silk scarf, letting the breeze ripple it invitingly.

The girl he was addressing gave the scarf a longing look, but shook her head, backing away from the table. Just that hesitation had cost her—she looked around, frantic for a moment, and then hurried to catch up with the woman who, not realizing that her companion had stopped, strode through the crowded flea market several paces ahead. The woman's gaze darted back and forth, scanning the crowd as though she was looking for someone—or looking to avoid someone.

"Libby?" the girl called, her voice high and thin with worry.

Elizabeth stopped, looking back with alarm that subsided when she saw her sister was not in trouble. "Maggie, come on! Stay with me, baby." Elizabeth's voice was calm and soft, but it carried through the crowd, and there was a note of tension running through it that her sister heard as clearly as a shout, and obeyed immediately.

"I'm sorry," Maggie said, running forward and slipping her hand into her sister's. "I'll stay close, I promise."

The two girls were obviously related; both of them were slender, with long legs, although the preteen Maggie's were more coltish than her older sister's. Long black hair, braided in Maggie's case and pulled into a long ponytail for Elizabeth, and wide-set brown eyes with a vaguely exotic cast, further stamped the family resemblance. Their looks hinted at Spanish blood, or Arabic: an exotic edge that spoke of distant lands and warmer climates than their current New England location. Although they wore plain jeans and unadorned sweatshirts, and Maggie had the same backpack over her shoulder as half the kids around her, something more than their looks set them apart from the others milling around them; something obvious, but difficult to identify.

It was a way of looking around, of observing without being part of the crowd, a difference that identified them—if an observer knew—as residents of an enclave that some cynics called a cult, or a commune, but most people simply called the Community.

Good folk, neighbors would say if asked. Founded, oh, near fifty years ago, wasn't it? Bunch of them came and bought old farmland, built it up nice with houses and gardens and a proper downtown with stores and whatnot. Pay their taxes on time, send their kids to the local schools, mostly. They don't seem to like technology much, but otherwise perfectly normal. Not a cult at all, no. No, there was nothing particularly strange about the Community.

Six months ago, Elizabeth would have agreed with them. Now, she was less certain.

"We have to hurry," she told Maggie. "They saw us come in here, but they can't keep track of us so long as we keep moving."

Maggie nodded, and the two moved on, weaving through the shoppers and sellers, moving around the overladen tables and backed-in vans that filled the parking lot of the makeshift flea market.

"Here, this way." They slipped behind an oversized van near the end of one row, between two racks of brightly tie-dyed summer dresses, and found themselves at the far end of the lot. Behind them, the bustle and noise of a warm Saturday afternoon. In front of them, a muddy field, cars parked in a squared-off pattern. To their left was the bulk of the local regional high school, a redbrick-and-chrome building. To their right, a large and dense-looking wooded area, green with new spring undergrowth and full-branched evergreens, enclosed by a mesh fence with official-looking signs posted at regular intervals. There was one place where the mesh was torn, exactly the right size for a high school student—or a slender adult—to slip through.

Elizabeth studied the distance between them and the fence, and then looked down at her sister. "Do you think you can make it, baby?"

Maggie set her jaw, judging the distance, then nodded. "Just keep up," she said with bravado that Elizabeth knew was faked. Her sister had been sick recently, her body wasn't as strong as it used to be. She got tired too easily now, needed more rest, more often. But they couldn't afford to rest, not yet.

"Just nonchalantly at first," her sister advised. "Walk like you're just stretching your legs, no hurry, no worries, okay? Come on, follow me."

They stepped out off the pavement, the muddy grass sucking at their shoes, their backpacks slung over their shoulders casually, as though they were just walking back to their car after a morning of shopping.

"Going somewhere, Libby?"

The two girls stopped cold, Elizabeth instinctively putting her arm around her younger sister as though to protect her from the man walking toward them. Damn.

A flicker of movement caught her eye, and she saw two other men circling around them, as though to herd them somewhere. Somewhere they definitely did not want to be.

Maggie let her backpack slide down her arm, taking the weight in her hand as though to use it as a weapon if need be, and shifted her weight, mimicking her sister's movement.

"Really, Libby," the first man said, exuding compassion. "Look at poor Maggie, she's exhausted. Don't do this to her. Why don't you tell us what's wrong? We're your family, we'll help you. Isn't that how it's always been?"

Elizabeth's shoulders tensed, but she otherwise didn't move. "Go to hell, Jordan. You're no family of mine." All of her family, save Maggie, were dead.

"Oh, Libby." Jordan was in his late forties, a handsome man in jeans and a dark blue polo shirt. He could have been someone's father, heading to a soccer game or baseball practice. But his gaze was intent, steady and cool, like that of a jailer. "Why do you insist on doing this? Come home with us. I know that losing your parents was a shock—"

"Leave my parents out of this." The pain of that loss was still bone-deep, six months later, but it only made her more determined to go nowhere with these three. "If they knew what was going on…"

Jordan looked hurt and surprised. "Elizabeth, nothing is going on! Nothing except this foolishness. Please, my dear. It's been a terribly stressful time, everyone knows that, but you're overreacting. Let us take care of you, you and Maggie both."

The other two men moved closer, blocking any chance of escaping into the crowd. They were dressed like Jordan in weekend-casual clothing, sturdy hiking boots under their jeans. If it came to running, Elizabeth and Maggie, in sneakers, might be able to escape…if they could run at top speed. Elizabeth didn't let herself look at her sister, didn't dare glance down at the leg that was still weak, after her bout with the terrible illness that had taken their parents earlier that year. She would not show fear, not in front of these men.

But the truth was there. Maggie would never be able to keep up.

Maggie leaned in against her sister, so that an observer might assume she was seeking reassurance— or offering it. "I can do it," she whispered, as though knowing exactly what her sister was thinking. Knowing Maggie, she did. Her sister was only thirteen, but she knew far too much, for her age. "I don't want to go back with them."

Elizabeth took a deep breath, still holding Jordan's gaze. Neither of them were going back. The thought of the sleepy little village where they had grown up, once the source of only happy memories, was enough to make Elizabeth ill. There was only death and fear there, now.

She gauged the distance again, and her heart sank.

Maggie, she thought, as hard as she could. *Maggie, be ready....*

Jordan saw both their gazes flicker toward the trees, and shook his head sadly. "Elizabeth. Maggie. Don't be idiots. You'd never make it, and then we'd all be out of breath and cranky. That's not good. Our van is right over there, why don't we walk over there like civilized people, and let the Elders sort all this unpleasantness out?"

"The Elders can bite me," Elizabeth said through gritted teeth. Before he could respond, she darted toward Jordan as though intending to tackle him. He flinched, and she pivoted away from him, daring him to catch her, even as Maggie was sprinting for the dubious safety of the woods. *Good girl,* Elizabeth thought. *Good girl, run!*

Even as she cheered inwardly, one of the other men lunged at Maggie as she went past him, grabbing her by the elbow and jerking her off her feet.

"Get your hands off her!" All thoughts of distracting Jordan fled, and Elizabeth went after the man holding her sister, intent only on freeing her from that hard grip. She had barely taken two steps when her arms were caught behind her back, stopping her forward motion and preventing her from taking further action. She swore, and struggled, trying to free herself.

Jordan's breath was warm in her ear as he said, gently, "There's no need to make a fuss, Elizabeth. Just—"

Elizabeth had no intention of going, quietly or otherwise. Leaning forward with all of her weight so that he had to lean back to steady himself, she gave a quick prayer that his grip would hold, and then kicked back with both feet, aiming up for his groin. The move sent her off balance, as expected, but she landed a solid blow and had the satisfaction of hearing him grunt in pain, and feeling his grip on her weaken. But her satisfaction was short-lived as he grabbed her long ponytail with a hand and yanked hard enough to bring tears to her eyes.

"Stupid, Elizabeth. Very, very stupid." All pretense of gentleness gone, he nodded curtly to the third man, who went off, Elizabeth assumed, to get their car. The man who had grabbed Maggie now had his arm around her neck in a choke hold. Their pose might, from a distance, look like a friendly roughhouse move, older brother to bratty little sister, except for the white-faced expression of fear on Maggie's face. Elizabeth felt her heart racing painfully, and all she could think was that she had failed; failed her parents, failed her sister, failed everyone and everything important to her.

An ordinary-looking black van pulled up to the edge of the parking lot, its wheels churning the grass into more mud, and the driver got out and slid open the side doors. Nobody seemed to notice, going about their buying and selling and socializing like it was any normal weekend. Maggie's eyes closed, and she looked like she was about to pass out.

Elizabeth's heart squeezed tight, and a sense of panic

swamped her, worse than the pain of her hair still being held fast in Jordan's fist. She could not allow them to take Maggie. Whatever else happened, she could not let them have her sister.

Trying to dig her heels into the mud, she prepared herself to make another attempt to get free, now that it was two against two. The odds were still bad, but she had no choice. Once they were in the van…

Even as she was trying not to imagine what would happen then, there was a thudding noise, distant but coming closer rapidly, as though a lone drummer had gotten lost from his band and was heading their way. The noise shouldn't have even registered, and yet it set up an answering reverberation in her bones, starting in her spine and sliding down to her knees. Rather than making them weak, though, it seemed almost to give her strength.

It also distracted Jordan. He swore, and the grip on her hair loosened so that Elizabeth was able to turn her head just enough to see a huge white form barreling from the trees, heading straight for the man holding Maggie.

The drumming filled her ears until she could hear nothing else, not the buzz from the crowded flea market behind them or Jordan's cursing, and all she could see was the inevitable impact about to happen.

Sure enough, the white form slammed into the two figures even as Elizabeth cried out in horror. The man went sprawling, the white figure rearing over it, coming down with hooves—hooves, it was a horse—even as Maggie rolled out of the way; free, if muddy.

Maggie was safe.

Sound came back in a rush, and Elizabeth heard Jordan shouting an order to the man driving the van, and felt him reach for something at his back. A gun? A phone? She couldn't take the chance. She used her elbows and the back of her head, ignoring the tearing pain of her hair being yanked out long enough to scramble free, falling onto her hands and knees in the muddy grass. She looked up, pushing the tangles of her hair from her eyes, and saw the horse pivot on its hind legs away from the now-downed man and come after Jordan, ignoring her completely.

"Maggie?" She scrambled forward and gathered her sister to her, then got them both to their feet. "Sweetie, run!"

Her sister, the knees and butt of her jeans now covered in mud and grass stains, managed to scramble forward and start running, Elizabeth staying just behind her in case she fell. She would carry Maggie, if that's what it took.

They'd only managed a few yards when the drumming noise got louder behind them. Elizabeth let herself take one look back, and saw the white horse come up alongside them, slowing down to keep pace with them. Somehow, instinctively, her hand was grabbing at the coarse hairs of the horse's mane, and pulling herself up onto its back in a move she'd read about in books, but had never done herself before now. The horse's back was broad, and her legs ached immediately from the effort of staying on, but she managed it, however gracelessly.

The horse moved forward, reaching Maggie, who had not paused in her flight. Elizabeth put down a hand, and Maggie grabbed it, like they had practiced the move for years, and she hauled her sister up. The horse checked itself midstride until Maggie was safe, clinging to her waist, and then lengthened its stride again.

And then they were traveling impossibly fast, the drumbeats sounding beneath them, hooves muffled against the ground, leaving Jordan and his companion behind. Elizabeth ducked forward against the thick neck of the horse, pulling Maggie with her and flinching in anticipation of bullets from the gun Jordan might have had. The warm, musty smell of the horse reached her nose, bringing an odd sort of comfort, and then she felt the muscles underneath her bunch up, tensing in anticipation of something....

Instinct and a distant sense of anticipation made her clench her legs even tighter around the horse's barrel-shaped ribs, and cling to the thick mane under her fingers, even as Maggie strengthened her grip around her waist and the horse's ears flicked forward, intent on the fence ahead of them.

And then the tensed muscles released, and the horse lifted as though, for an instant, they were flying, sheer power taking them over the mesh fence and landing with a surprisingly soft, if jarring, thud of hooves

against dirt. Elizabeth barely had time to release a surprised "whoof" of breath before they were out of the
open air and into the cool, shaded depths of the woods.

Within minutes, the sounds of civilization faded, replaced by the occasional burst of birdsong that paused
as they passed, and then started up again. The horse's
gallop changed to a steady, almost careful trot, but Elizabeth kept her face down and her hands tight in the
horse's mane, acutely aware of her sister's arms around
her waist. She didn't dare look up or try to control the
horse, for fear of dislodging that precious, precarious
cargo, or falling off herself. Her legs were sore from
gripping the animal's sides, and her arms ached from
holding on, and her scalp stung from where Jordan had
pulled her hair, but all she could think was *don't fall off.
Don't let Maggie fall off.*

Her heartbeat slowed slowly, her breathing less
raspy-sounding in her own ears, but the fear remained
a constant, expecting any moment to hear Jordan's voice
shouting behind them, the roar of the van as it tried to
follow them. But with every stride forward they took,
and the lengthening of silence, Elizabeth dared hope
that they had made good their escape.

The trees were thicker together now, and the horse
had slowed to a cautious walk, allowing Elizabeth to
relax her legs a little, and sit up enough to see where
they were going. They were following what looked like
a deer path—she didn't dare twist to look behind her,

but it was unlikely anything wider than the horse would be able to follow them. If Jordan and his men came, they would have to do so on foot, and they could not keep up with a horse, even if they managed to get past that fence.

For the moment, they were free.

"You okay, baby?" she asked.

"Yeah." Her sister's voice came back, shaken but strong. The arms around her waist gave a reassuring squeeze. "I might throw up once my stomach catches up with us, though."

That made Elizabeth laugh a little, the way Maggie intended. Her sister was always there with a joke or tease, no matter how bad things got. It was one of her many gifts.

The ground sloped downward slightly, and then evened out into a clearing. The horse, tired, or just finally bored with carrying riders, stopped, its head dropping low. The message was clear: end of the trip. Elizabeth felt Maggie slide off, and, once she was certain her sister was safe on the ground, unclenched her fingers from the mane and swung her leg over the horse's back, sliding carefully down to the ground. The horse stood steady throughout, and she patted it on the neck, feeling a layer of sweat on the surprisingly soft, warm skin. "Thank you."

The horse snorted as though it understood, and she stepped away, testing her wobbly legs and trying to hear if there were any sounds of pursuit.

The only noises were birds twittering and calling in

the branches overhead, and the quiet trickle of water somewhere nearby. Maggie, contrary to her threat, was not throwing up. Elizabeth stood still and let out a deep breath. It wasn't safety, not really, but it was closer than she'd felt in months.

"Where are we?" Maggie asked, looking around in wonder at the huge trees surrounding them.

Elizabeth had to stop and think for a moment. They'd ridden their bikes from home, and abandoned them by a middle school in the hopes that someone would take them and muddy the trail. Obviously, that hadn't worked. They'd walked west from there, the rest of the morning, and had ducked into the flea market to get something to eat when she'd caught sight of Jordan following them. In the mad dash after, she hadn't been paying too much attention to the surroundings, but...

"I think it's a reservoir preserve," she said. "State land." If so, that was better than she had hoped for—the treed area would be large enough that they should be able to evade being observed, at least until she figured out their next move. And even if there was a road through it, only state vehicles would be allowed in. Hiding in here would give them a little time to breathe. She didn't think she had really relaxed since the day before, when the notice from the Elders had come.

Being summoned before the Elders wasn't a huge deal—it could have been anything, from wanting to discuss the plans she had submitted six months before to enlarge the bakery she owned, or discussing what would happen to the house she had shared with her parents, now that they were gone. It was too large for only two people, and there were others in the Community who could have used the space. That was all the normal course of events, the sort of thing the Elders would summon her to discuss.

But she had known, the moment she opened the envelope, that it had been none of those things. She wasn't gifted the way Maggie was, but she'd had a dream the night before, and the sense of menace had been centered on a white square of paper—the same paper she held in her hands, mere hours later.

Her parents were dead, victims of the terrible flu that had swept through the Community at the beginning of the winter. Cody—her best friend—was dead, just a week past. One by one, everything, everyone who mattered, had been taken from them. She didn't know why, but she knew it for a fact; and that Ray, who led the Elders, was at the heart of it. Ray wanted Maggie for himself.

Her dreams were certain of that. They just didn't know why.

"So where did you come from, big guy?" Caught in her memories, Elizabeth barely listened to her sister talking to the horse, until the younger girl let out a gasp.

"Maggie? Wha—"

She turned and looked at her sister—and by inclusion, looked at the horse, too.

It was white, she had noted that already. Sleek and

muscled, as tall at the shoulder as she was, with a thick golden-white tail and shaggy mane, and large brown eyes looking directly at her, a darker golden forelock falling over its forehead and above that…

Above that…

Her brain stopped, refusing to formulate the thought, refusing to acknowledge what she was seeing.

"Libby." Maggie's voice, hushed with awe. "It has a horn!"

Chapter 2

Once Elizabeth caught her breath, she said the first thing that came into her brain.

"There is no such thing as a unicorn."

The words sounded perfectly reasonable, and sane, and confident. Considering that her sister had her arm around the neck of a horse—very definitely a horse—with a foot-long, spiral-shaped, pointed horn in the middle of its forehead, Elizabeth wasn't sure she believed her own words. But she repeated them anyway. "There is no such thing as a unicorn. It has to be a fake, some kind of a con or scam. Or it's a mutant deer."

It didn't look anything like a deer, or a moose, or even a mule. It was definitely a horse. And that was definitely a horn.

So it had to be a fake. If she touched the horn it would be plaster, or plastic, somehow glued onto the horse's head. Or grafted, some kind of surgical measure… Who would do such a thing? A circus or a sideshow? Maybe. That was the most reasonable guess. Sideshows did that kind of thing all the time, didn't they? She had been to one, once, when Maggie was very little, a traveling circus, with cotton candy and carnival rides. They'd had a bearded woman and a so-called mermaid in a tank, so a unicorn would fit perfectly.

Yes. That made sense. Elizabeth nodded once, satisfied. If it belonged to a circus, no matter if the horn was fake or a freak of nature, then it was probably valuable. There might even be a reward, but no matter how much they were going to need money, they couldn't afford to take advantage. They needed to stay out of sight, away from anyone's attention, until she had time to think things through, and figure out what to do.

And if it was a scam of any sort, they really couldn't afford to be caught up in it. Especially not if the person who was running it came looking for his or her animal, causing trouble. Elizabeth would go to the police, if she had to, but not as part of someone else's problems. They'd take Maggie away from her for sure, then.

And if they took Maggie away, it would be easy for Ray, as an Elder, to claim custody. Elizabeth knew, bone-deep, that if he did that, she would never be allowed near her sister again, that Maggie would never be free. There was no evidence to support that—Ray had never done or said anything threatening—but she *knew*.

But the only people who might have believed her were dead, now. Only she was left to protect Maggie.

Her sister, not sharing her worries, was busy petting the creature, cooing into pointed white ears that flickered back and forth as she spoke.

"Maggie…be careful," she warned, watching the horn come dangerously close to her sister's body as the horse leaned into the hug. Even if it was fake, that tip was probably sharp.

"It won't hurt us," Maggie said, stubbornly hugging the beast. "It helped us! Didn't you, guy?" She rested her face against the white neck. "You saved us. Like Prince Charming's noble steed. Only where did you leave Prince Charming?"

The horse made a noise like a snort, and shoved Maggie—gently, but enough to make her stagger, as though responding to her question with indignation.

"Maggie, please step away from the horse. I agree, it helped us, but it's still a strange animal and outweighs you by a considerable amount." Her sister had never met an animal that she couldn't charm, but Elizabeth saw no reason to tempt fate.

Maggie made a face, but complied, giving the beast one last pat before taking several steps away. The horse watched her, but stayed where it was. "You think they'll find us again?" Her voice was matter-of-fact, but her body tensed as she spoke.

Elizabeth wanted nothing more than to reassure the younger girl that everything would be all right, that they were safe, but she had never directly lied to her little sister, not in thirteen years, and she wasn't going to start now. "Not if we're smart. We need to figure out how to get to the other side of the reservoir, somehow, and then we can find a bus station. Once we're farther away, they won't be able to find us again."

She hoped. Her only plan had been to get as far away from the Community as possible, and find someone who wasn't cowed by Ray, someone who would listen to them, and protect them. But now... Elizabeth looked around, noting that the light that had been slanting through the trees was fading, all too aware of the fact that they had no idea where they were—any direction she chose could lead them right back into Jordan's clutches, or leave them wandering deeper into the woods, away from the bus station that was their only chance to get away.

Jordan was a smarmy bastard, but he was right—Maggie was still exhausted. She needed to rest, and have a good meal, something more than the hot dogs they had gotten at the flea market, and...things they weren't going to find, standing here like ninnies. Elizabeth mentally counted the money they had left, and flinched. There was enough for bus tickets out of state, and another meal or three, but not much more than that.

"I just need to figure out which way leads to the next town over." She didn't even know what town they were in right now. She had lived here her entire life, all twenty-six years, and once she got outside a ten-mile radius of her home, she was lost. What the hell had she been thinking, abandoning everything without a plan?

Panicked. She had been panicked, and knew, the same way that she knew the summons was bad news, that Ray was counting on her to be her usual practical, pragmatic self. Think-it-through Libby, her dad always called her. Think-it-through Libby would never have yanked her sister out of school and abandoned everything they owned on an hour's notice, on the basis of a series of bad dreams and a gut feeling.

But she had.

The horse took two steps forward, so graceful it seemed almost to float more than walk, and, bypassing Maggie, circled around Elizabeth. She turned to watch it move, only to stagger herself when it pushed at her from behind with its shoulder. She had been right; it was solid muscle, and she had to take several steps forward to keep from falling over.

Up close, the horn was clearly attached to the forehead with more than glue, and when she—with daring that amazed her—reached out to touch it, the sensation under her fingertips was that of solid bone, smooth and cool and heavy.

With that touch, a wall of memories fell on her. She could almost hear her mother's laugh, see Cody's bright, fearless smile, smell the scent of her dad's cologne….

No. Those were memories of better times, happier

times. If she let them come back now, she would break down and then Maggie would be lost.

The horse, as though sensing her thoughts, stepped closer, pushing her again with the exact same amount of force behind the shove, and she got a definite sense of being told to get a move on.

"That way?" She felt insane, asking an animal for directions, but…maybe not so insane, after all. She looked at Maggie, who was looking at the beast intently. Her sister nodded.

"I think so. It wants us to go…that way?" Maggie pointed in the direction the horse—the unicorn, all right, Elizabeth admitted it, the unicorn—was pushing her.

It shoved her again, and she took the third step of her own accord, almost numb at this point. "What the hell. You got us here, maybe you can get us out."

There was so much that was crazy in her life, what was taking directions from a unicorn, at this point? The thought almost made her laugh. Almost.

Maggie slipped her hand into her sister's, and they walked forward along the indentation in the grass that indicated a deer path, the unicorn following behind. Its hooves barely made any noise on the dirt, now that it was walking rather than galloping. Elizabeth glanced behind, unable to help herself, and those wide brown eyes met hers in an almost human glance. It was taller than they were, its head above their shoulders, so it would be able to see anything coming ahead of them.

More, its chest was broad and muscled, and its hooves were weapons able to take out anything coming up from behind them. *Trust me,* that dark gaze seemed to say.

The sense of safety she had felt earlier returned, and she nodded once in response, and then turned her attention back to the barely visible track winding through the trees.

They walked in silence a few strides, but Elizabeth could feel something building within her normally sunny-tempered sister. She waited, patiently, and finally it burst out.

"They're not going to give up, are they? Why, Libby? Why won't they just let us alone?"

All Elizabeth had told her sister as a reason for their flight was that the Elders wanted to separate them, place Maggie in another household, a real family, not just a sister who worked too many hours to raise a teenager. Elizabeth hadn't mentioned any of her other fears, the ones that seemed insane in the daylight, but so very real when shadows surrounded them. Cody might have been able to banish the fears, with his laughter and his optimism, but Cody had hung himself on the tree behind his house, six days ago. Eight days after Elizabeth had confided her dream-stirred worries to him.

Maggie knew, anyway. Maggie always knew. Like Elizabeth's dreams, only more so. Maggie Sweet was special that way.

"I don't know," Elizabeth said now, in response to the question. "I wish I did, but I don't. We'll stay together, baby. Just like I promised you." When their parents had died, at the shared grave among so many other graves, she had sworn that she would always be there, that she would not leave Maggie alone.

"Okay." As simple as that, and to Maggie, the world was right side up and stable. Elizabeth wished, not for the first time, that she had her sister's faith in her own abilities.

Cody had told her once that, if she put her mind to it, she could grow wings and fly. But Cody was dead. The police, called in from the nearest town, said he had committed suicide, too depressed by the spate of deaths in the Community to go on. Elizabeth knew better. No matter what, no matter how many friends they lost, he would never have done that, would never have gone without a word to her. Not after what she'd confessed to him. But nobody would believe her, thinking her stressed and grief-stricken.

If she had insisted, if she had uttered a single word about her fears, her dreams of something terrible about to happen, Ray would have had all the excuse he needed to take Maggie away from her.

Elizabeth didn't know how long or how far they walked, but her feet were beginning to hurt, and Maggie was clearly fading.

"We're going deeper in, not out," her sister said, her fingers tightening around Elizabeth's hand. "Is that okay? Shouldn't we be going out?"

"I think it's taking us around the reservoir," Elizabeth said. "It must…smell water, or something. Or maybe it's going back to its stable…it's okay, Maggie. We don't want to go back the way we came, so anything is better than that, right? Look, see those yellow flowers? They're called lady's slippers. They're orchids. Do you remember? Mom had a pillow she'd made, it had those embroidered on it."

Maggie scrunched her face, trying to remember. "It was green? On the rocking chair?"

"That's right. The dog ate it, when you were, oh, about nine."

"Poor Mickey." The memory, as she'd hoped, made her sister laugh, and forget her exhaustion for a while. "He always ate everything, and Mom would get so mad…. I miss them, Libby. I miss them so much."

Elizabeth's heart ached. "So do I, baby."

Their parents hadn't been young—Maggie was a surprise late child—but the flu epidemic that swept the Community shouldn't have taken them, not both of them, healthy adults still in their prime. So many people who should not have died, and yet they had, young children and adults alike.

Six months since those deaths, and the pain was still as raw as if the funeral had been yesterday. How much worse was it for Maggie, almost fourteen years younger, without the memories to console her? Elizabeth did her best, with photographs and stories, but eventually it would all be a faded blur, especially now that the photographs, like everything else, had been left behind. Elizabeth had taken a few photos, quickly pulled from frames and stuffed into her bag, but it wasn't enough, not nearly enough.

Stories would have to fill the gap.

"You were too young to remember, the year that Mickey tried to jump the fire with everyone else during Winterfair. He almost made it, too, except his tail drooped too much, and he got all singed. You've never seen such an embarrassed-looking dog, his tail all bandaged, so every time he wagged it, he swatted someone...."

The stories flowed from her as they walked, the smell of warm dirt and pine in the air, the pine needles and dirt soft underfoot. It couldn't have been all that long, in reality—maybe two hours, if that, since they'd been approached by Jordan and his men—but the light kept fading, the angle of the setting sun not making its way through the tall branches, until it became difficult to see where they were going. Maggie was leaning against her more than before, and she was about to tell her to get back on the horse's back, when it tapped her—gently, carefully—on the shoulder with its horn, and then nudged her off to the left.

They left the path, faint as it was, and walked through a line of trees and down a small decline. Up ahead, as though waiting for them, there was a clearing, about ten feet in circumference, where the tall evergreens formed an almost perfect circle. Inside the circle there was a pile of leaves and soft branches piled in the middle.

"It looks like a bed," Maggie said. "I think we're supposed to sleep here?"

Elizabeth looked back at the horse, who stared back at her. "It's not exactly Motel Six."

"A lot cheaper," Maggie said, for once being the practical one. "And we're here." She knelt down in the pile, testing it with her hand. "It's actually soft," she said, surprised. "And dry."

"Is this where you sleep?" Elizabeth asked the horse, and then felt like a proper idiot. It might have a horn, and it might be leading them somewhere, but expecting it to suddenly answer her... She needed sleep as much as Maggie did, clearly. She hadn't slept, really slept, in almost a week. Certainly not since they'd cut Cody's body down from the tree.

"Thank you," she said to the horse, anyway. "For... everything."

Maggie was busy arranging their knapsacks to act as pillows, trying different positions to see if she could see the sky through the branches overhead. She was clearly taken with the idea of spending the night out of doors.

Sleeping in the woods wasn't Elizabeth's idea of comfort, but it was smart. Jordan wouldn't stop looking, but he only had a few people with him, and searching the entire forest would take too long, especially since it would be dark soon. He couldn't afford to bring in more people, or ask for help, since they would want to avoid any official attention as much as she did. Maybe even more. Cody's death had been investigated by the police, if briefly. Having his best friend turn up missing a week after his death might send up official warning flags, make someone outside the Community take notice.

Anyway, nobody would believe that she'd keep Maggie outside all night, not when she'd been so sick. Jordan would be looking for her in town, under shelter. If they could sleep here, and get started early in the morning, when he'd be asleep, they could maybe slip past him.

It was the best plan she could come up with. And Maggie was already curled up in the makeshift nest, half-asleep from exhaustion but still trying to see stars through the overhead canopy of leaves. Elizabeth took off her jacket and draped it over the younger girl, then curled up next to her, snuggling for comfort. Maggie was right, it was surprisingly soft and comfortable. As her eyes closed, almost against her will, the last sight she had was their rescuer, a pale glimmer in the dusk, standing guard, his head up and alert to any sound or movement beyond the circle.

Reassured and oddly comforted by the sight, she slept.

Ever since the first wave of flu deaths hit the Community back in the autumn, Elizabeth's dreams had been filled with faceless shadows moving around her, the sense of being caught in a whirlpool, spinning her around and pulling her down to some dire fate. It was all silent, as though the sound had been sucked out of the world already, except for her sister's breath, labored and wet. It was the sound of a flu victim, trying to breathe, and no matter how terrifying the dream, waking to hear that noise in reality terrified Elizabeth more. Even now, when Maggie looked like the picture of health, the slightest hitch in her breath or faintest cough sent Elizabeth into a vague panic.

She had always dreamed, and always remembered her dreams, even as a small child. When something good was going to happen, or something bad, or merely a change in the air—she had known that her mother was pregnant with Maggie weeks before her mother realized, and had known that the small baby growing there would change her life forever. But she had never had nightmares—not until almost a year ago, when she woke screaming with the sense that something was lurking, just out of sight, waiting to catch her, to rend her apart with its claws. Nothing concrete, no specifics—only with Maggie's birth had she ever known what change was coming, specifically. Only a sense of dread and distress that she could not shake, and could not prevent.

When her parents died, Elizabeth expected the nightmares to stop. Instead, they intensified. The night before Cody's death, the dreams had been even worse: Maggie's pale face alternating with Cody's laughing one, and then her parents cold in their coffins, and a sense of menace no longer lurking in the shadows, but in midleap, claws outstretched. She had woken, not screaming but crying, her chest burning as though she'd been running all night, and been unable to go back to sleep. She had lain in bed for hours, waiting for the sun to come up, until the message came that Cody had been found, dead. She had not truly slept since then, unable to relax even in her own bed.

Tonight, curled up under a roof of trees while armed men searched for them, effectively homeless, guarded by an impossible creature and the future terrifyingly uncertain, Elizabeth slept, and dreamed not of menace, but of joy. In her dream, she stood under an open vista of clear blue skies and white-capped mountains, and felt the presence of peace and love around her, embracing her.

It was somewhere she had never been, a peace she never felt even in the best of times. Yet even within the embrace of that peace there was an uncertainty inside her, a sense that something would go wrong; that this contentment wasn't meant for her. Not if she couldn't take care of Maggie, make sure that Maggie was safe.

The dream faded, and she felt herself waking up in slow, comfortable stages: the warm crackle of their bedding underneath, the faint dampness of dew on her skin and clothing, the reassuring sound of Maggie's occasional sleep-snort and the press of her body still curled under Elizabeth's protective arm. Maggie was still safe. For now.

The light was dim around them, filtered through the leaves and barely enough to see by. Elizabeth guessed it was a little before dawn. At home, before everything changed, this had been her favorite time of day; before the controlled chaos of opening the bakery and getting the day's orders started. Libby's Loaves had been her own domain, her contribution to the Community at large. How proud she had been of it!

Her mother had taught her how to bake bread, back when she was Maggie's age. There was another bakery in the Community, but it was Libby's Loaves that everyone wanted for their table—she left the pastries and cakes to Asha and her husband, who owned the other shop across town.

She hoped they understood the meaning of the recipes—and the deed—she had left under their door, just before she and Maggie had left.

Those thoughts led to the awareness that they needed to be up and moving soon, and no time for reminiscences or regrets. Sliding her arm away from Maggie carefully, to keep from waking her just yet, Elizabeth got up from their makeshift mattress and looked around to see if the horse had stayed with them, overnight, or had wandered off as mysteriously as it had appeared. They hadn't even thought to tether it—not that there had been anything to tether it with, since there had been neither bridle nor lead rope to use. Still…

The circle they had slept in was horse free. Elizabeth admitted to a sinking feeling of disappointment that didn't make any sense. Whatever the animal was—horse, deer, fake or real—it wasn't theirs, and while it had been amazingly, almost miraculously helpful, she couldn't count on that help continuing.

"Just you and me again, baby," she said, turning to wake Maggie and get her ready to walk again, and yelped in shock at the man standing across the clearing from her, watching her with a steady gaze.

Chapter 3

Her yelp woke Maggie in a rush, the teenager sitting upright and looking automatically in the direction her sister was staring. Maggie let out a startled noise as well, scooting backward on her knees to where her sister stood, instinctively seeking protection from this stranger. Fleetingly Elizabeth rued the loss of the little girl who was open and friendly to everyone, even as she was putting herself between this unknown man and her sister.

Better that Maggie be cautious. Better that Maggie be safe.

"Who the hell are you?" she asked, trying to see if there was anyone creeping up behind them without taking her eyes off the immediate threat. He wasn't very tall, with broad shoulders and a wide-set stance that made her think of gunslingers in old Western movies, and was dressed in faded black jeans and a dark red pullover. His hair was honey-blond, his skin tanned, as though he spent most of his time outdoors, and his eyes, watching her, were a deep, dark brown that stirred something in her, some sense of familiarity, of long-lost comfort. She distrusted the feeling immediately.

"Hush," the stranger said, in a voice that was low and raspy, as though he was recovering from a sore throat, or didn't speak often. "Those men are in the woods, looking for you again, and your shrieks carry like a siren."

Elizabeth felt her jaw drop open, and then closed it again with a snap. The worried look in those eyes softened the harshness of his words, and the fact that he knew what was happening, and seemed intent on helping them…

Her ability to trust had been severely strained over the past few months, and there was nothing that said this man was any different than Jordan and his cronies, but…she had to make a choice right then and there. She chose to trust him.

"It's all right, Maggie," she said as quietly as she could. "Just be still."

The stranger stood there, listening to something, then all of a sudden he seemed to relax, and Elizabeth felt herself breathing more easily, too.

"They've gone back to their cars," he said, as though

talking to himself, not them. "Getting you out of here is going to be tricky, now, but staying isn't going to work, either." His already square jaw firmed even more in annoyance. "Damn it, I don't have time for this. If I get you out of here, you're on your own."

Elizabeth wanted to make a sarcastic retort to that, but she was still too shocked, and afraid to antagonize the one person who had been willing to help them, whatever his reasons.

"Who are you?" Maggie asked. "Do...do we know you?" Her voice had an expectant quality, as though half hoping for a reassuring response.

The man hesitated, as though not wanting to answer, and then grinned. It wasn't a friendly grin, or a reassuring one. "We met last night."

"We met..." Elizabeth stared at him blankly, and then Maggie shrieked in excitement, immediately clapping her hands over her mouth when they both looked down, horrified at the noise.

"You were... Oh, my God, you were the unicorn!"

"Maggie, don't be ridiculous," Elizabeth said automatically, even as her sister got to her feet and walked toward the stranger.

"You are, aren't you? That is so cool, totally amaze!"

Even as she was shaking her head, trying to come up with some other explanation, Elizabeth was amused at her sister's words. For a while there, before the flu struck, everything had been "amaze." "Totally amaze" was Maggie's highest praise.

"Are you a unicorn who turns into a man, or a man who turns into a unicorn? I think you're prettier as a unicorn."

Elizabeth bit back a grin at the man's rather startled and somewhat annoyed reaction to her sister's artless question and statement. She didn't agree at all with Maggie's assessment—the horse had been a handsome animal but the man was…well, he was a handsome animal, too, she admitted.

"Maggie. That was rude."

Her sister looked at her, eyes wide. "How is it rude?"

"Ah…" She looked helplessly at the stranger, who scowled back at her. "Men aren't pretty. They're handsome." They also didn't magically transfer from man to horse, or back again, but knocking Maggie's fantasy would be cruel, right now. If that was how she dealt with the stress, it was harmless enough. He seemed willing to go along with it, despite the scowl, so that was either a point in his favor or really creepy—and that still didn't get to the question of how this man knew them, or…

"Was the horse yours? We're terribly sorry, we didn't mean… It appeared when we needed it—we would have returned it, if we knew where it came from…."

There was no way that she was going to explain to this man how his horse had literally rescued them. She knew what had happened, but the words couldn't come out of her mouth.

"Libby, I told you! He *is* the unicorn!"

"Maggie…" It was one thing to indulge Maggie's

fantasies, but Elizabeth wasn't sure how far she wanted to go with that.

"It's true! You know I know!"

Maggie's voice had a strained, pleading quality to it. Her sister wasn't the sort to make up stories—she didn't need to. But this was asking too much for even Elizabeth to believe.

Josh fought down his growing irritation, unable to believe that he was standing there while two females argued over his identity. Hell, he couldn't believe that they were even having that argument. No sane human being could believe in unicorns at all, much less one that shifted between human and horse form; it was the stuff of legends and myths, not reality. Were they insane? Had he stumbled upon a pair of escapees from a mental hospital? If so, they were two seriously good-looking patients: the girl was still coltish and awkward, but her sister had an elegance that only added to her striking good looks. And those eyes... When she had turned and he'd gotten his first real look at those dark, almond-shaped eyes, something inside him had plummeted all the way from his head to his knees. He suspected it might have been his brain.

The last thing he needed in his life right now was complications—more complications, he amended ruefully—and time was wasting. He needed to be on his way. And yet, something had made him come to their rescue...and that something wouldn't let him leave them stranded here, even though every bit of horse sense he had was telling him to go, *now.*

He had spent all night standing watch over them, listening to them sleep, the way a herd stallion would watch over his mares. The need to protect them was still strong enough to override his own instinct for self-preservation, his need to be moving, to follow the tug in his gut before it destroyed him.

"Damn it, the last thing I need are two females on my back." Literally. Although they'd both stayed on quite well—long and lean, like natural riders. He felt a burn start at the thought of a woman riding him, and beat it down fiercely. Bad enough that he had to deal with this damnable *rut,* he wasn't going to let it overtake his larger head, too.

The rut demanded that he move, that he find his mate, and complete the natural cycle of the Mustang. So why had he come to help them, stayed with them— why the hell had he allowed them to see him in both forms? He was nearly thirty, old enough to know better, damn it, not act like some fool yearling.

"It's my fault," the younger one—Maggie—said suddenly, as though hearing his thoughts. "I called you."

"Maggie!"

The older girl—woman—sounded scandalized.

Maggie refused to be silenced. "He deserves to know, doesn't he? I didn't mean to, I was just so scared when those guys showed up, and then he was within reach, and..." The girl shrugged helplessly, and he revised his estimate of her age—she couldn't be more than twelve or thirteen. No wonder his instinct kicked in; she was barely a yearling herself. But what did she mean—called him?

"It's a gift," she said, hearing his thoughts again, somehow. "I've always been able to do it. Call animals, I mean. Libby doesn't want me to tell anyone, because people get scared, but you should know. Because I'm sorry. It's one thing to call an animal, but not a person. That's not polite."

Josh felt like someone had punched him in the chest. "You called me. Right." Nobody called him; he was broken to no damned halter. No Mustang ever answered to any call but their own desires.

"I did." She sounded almost insulted that he didn't believe her. "I didn't mean to, but you were there and you heard me, I guess. You don't believe me. That's okay, nobody ever does. Watch."

She turned away from him, a defiant tilt to her shoulders, and stared into the limbs of the tree above them. He turned to the older girl—a young woman, closer to his own age than her sister—but she was watching Maggie with a worried expression on her face. Because she was crazy, both of them were crazy? Or because the girl was about to do something that worried her? He turned back to watch the younger girl, waiting for an answer.

"There," Maggie said, speaking up into the tree. "Hello, little one. Come down here, please?"

He got the feeling that she was speaking out loud for

his benefit, not her own, and then all thought fled as a large reddish-brown squirrel jumped down from the branches and scurried across the ground to wait at Maggie's feet, beady black eyes bright, plump tail fluffed in anticipation, perched on its haunches as though awaiting further instructions.

"Be careful," he found himself warning her. "It might have rabies, or…"

"It doesn't," she said confidently, and bent down to pick the squirrel up. It not only allowed her to handle it, but the rodent also ducked its head under her hand as though anticipating a caress. He would have sworn it was a domesticated pet, except that there was no way…

"All right, Maggie," her sister said. She sounded tired, still worried, but amused at the same time. "You've proven your point. Now put greykins down—you know full well that even the gentle ones carry germs and ticks, and all sorts of things that you can't protect yourself from."

"Yes, ma'am," Maggie said, and let the squirrel go. It paused, as though disappointed, and then its natural caution resumed and it scampered up the nearest tree, an outraged chittering floating down back to them.

"It didn't like being summoned," he said dryly, his mood made worse, not better, by proof of her claims. He had been yanked off his course by a teenager's whim?

"Oh, it's just cranky," Maggie said airily. "Squirrels are always cranky. Are you? I'm sorry, I really am. I just never thought the animals minded so much, being summoned—they never seem to object." Her expression changed as she suddenly considered that they might, indeed, object.

"I'm not an animal." Was he annoyed? Josh thought that he might be, now that he'd had proof shoved in his face; this slip of a girl had managed to pull him away from his own agenda, tangling him up in whatever was going on with her and her sister without so much as a by-your-leave or pretty-please.

Still. Remembering the man who had been threatening them, the cruel grip on the woman's hair, the way the other man had twisted Maggie's arms...he couldn't regret coming to their aid, no matter how he had ended up there.

But it ended now. They were safe, and he had his own plans to follow through on. Plans that carried their own urgency.

"Maggie." The older girl, Libby, sat on a fallen tree trunk and shook her head at her sister in dismay. "You're hopeless."

Despite his annoyance, there was something about the older girl that intrigued him even more than her unusual sister. He eyed her carefully. Tall and lean, he had noted that already. Striking more than pretty. Lovely long dark hair past her shoulders, loosed from the ponytail, and now tangled with leaves and twigs like a dryad. Wide dark brown eyes and dusky skin, a full mouth and a proud Roman nose that was somehow more enchanting than any upturned pug or cute button could ever be. His gaze traveled lower. Her long-sleeved T-shirt didn't disguise a rounded chest, neither too large nor too small but just about right for cupping in his hands, and a long waist that tapered to hips his fingers itched to span. And those legs, stretched out in front of her...

He'd already felt how those legs felt, wrapped around him, her lower half molding to his as they moved. He'd had people—other women—on his back before, but they had mostly been his own herd, cousins and second cousins, the occasional human who knew their secret already. Never a stranger. Never a stranger with eyes that heated his imagination as much as his body.

"I don't suppose you're a virgin?" he asked suddenly.

Her jaw fell open, and a blush stained her cheeks, visible even in the morning light. "No."

She was quite certain about that and he shrugged inwardly. Oh, well. It had been a long shot, anyway.

"And you said *I* was rude?" Maggie asked, her eyes wide with astonishment.

He didn't explain why he had asked, but scowled at them again. "So why were those men after you, anyway?" He didn't care, really. But it was a way to put them on the defensive, rather than mocking him, or asking questions.

Libby stared at him, her scowl not quite a match for his own, but close. "We appreciate your assistance," she said, not answering the question, "but we need to be on our way now." Her tone was frostily polite, a verbal slap. "I don't suppose you could point us in the direction of the nearest police station? Then you can find your horse and be on your way."

Apparently, she was less convinced than her sister of his dual nature, or just determined to be contrary. Josh wasn't sure if he should be relieved or annoyed. Not that he went around announcing himself to strangers—to anyone—but he didn't like being doubted, either.

But this gave him the perfect excuse to leave. Why then, suddenly, did he not want to?

"Libby, I told you!" Maggie looked as though she was about to stomp her foot on the ground, very much like a frustrated yearling.

"Hush, child," he said. "Your sister is quite right, you two need to be on your way, before your hunters come back. I'll finish the job my…horse started, and get you out of the woods. But after that you're on your own, understand?" He looked at Maggie as he said that, and she nodded once in understanding. There would be no more summoning of him, however she had actually done it.

Did he believe that she could call animals, control them? Even if he denied that she had influenced him at all—he still wasn't comfortable with the idea—he had seen a sample for himself, and…really, who was he to question other people's oddities? The Mustang family was nothing more than legend and fairy tale to most folk, but he was quite real. A girl who could talk to the animals was commonplace, compared to his bloodline.

"There's a stream down that way—" He jerked his chin toward the slope. "You might want to wash up there, make yourself a little more presentable." Unable to stop himself, he reached out and plucked a twig from Libby's tangle of hair, holding it up in front of her face as evidence. "A comb or brush wouldn't hurt, either, if you have one."

She pursed her mouth as though about to say something, then shook her head and sighed, reaching down to pick up her backpack, a rugged olive-drab thing scuffed enough that it might have seen actual military service at some point. Maggie giggled, for the first time sounding like a girl her age, and picked up her own knapsack, a bright blue one that looked like it should be holding schoolbooks and lunch, not…whatever she had crammed in there. A toothbrush, he hoped.

He needed to reclaim his own pack, stashed in a tree when he had shifted to go to their rescue. Thankfully, clothing on his two-legged form merged into four-legged hide somehow, but the things they carried, even in pockets, the magic did not recognize. Even his wallet and spare change had to stay in his pack at all times, or risk being magicked out of existence. He was used to improvising, after a shift. He ran a tongue thoughtfully across his teeth, and grimaced. He really wished he had his toothbrush with him right now, though.

Libby took her sister's hand and led her through the circle of trees. He couldn't see them anymore but he could hear them—and scent them. If they ran into trouble, he could be there in an instant.

Not that he was still protecting them. Damn it.

* * *

"He's cute."

"Maggie, go dunk your head."

The stream wasn't deep enough to actually bathe in, and the water was cold enough to feel sharp against her skin, but Elizabeth washed her face and rinsed her mouth, rummaging in her bag for the travel kit she had shoved in there the day before. "And don't forget to brush your teeth."

He was cute, their grumpy rescuer. She was a breathing heterosexual female; she wasn't going to not notice that. But he was also clearly impatient to be rid of them, and she wasn't going to rely on a stranger, not when even those she'd called family had turned on them, the town she'd been raised in had gone dark and threatening. No, it would be best to take his help and then be gone themselves, as fast as possible.

Wash-up done as best she could, Elizabeth got out a brush and sat down to attack her tangled hair. Her father used to call her hair black silk, but right now it felt more like wool, rough and gritty, and in dire need of carding. Thankfully, once she picked out the leaves and twigs the worst of it was quickly tamed, and she braided it. Her sister's wash-up finished with considerably more splashing and face-making at the cold, and she motioned Maggie over to sit, cross-legged in front of her, while Elizabeth redid her braid in the same fashion. The stranger—she didn't even know his name!—

was right; they needed to look presentable, if they were going to try to make the police believe them.

That gave her pause, fingers holding three strands of hair motionless as she realized what she was planning. Was she really going to go to the police? She was, yes.

"Libby?"

"Yes, baby," she said, her fingers moving again, tying off the braid with a scrunchie from her pocket.

"He was the unicorn. He really was."

"Maggie…"

"He *was*."

She couldn't see her sister's face, but she could hear the halfhearted pout in the words. A man who changed into a unicorn. A were-unicorn?

Elizabeth tugged slightly on the braid, to indicate that she was done. Her baby sister talked to animals. She herself dreamed the future, however confused and clouded. Did she really have room to deny the possibility of weirder things out there?

"Then where were his clothes, when he changed? And…how can he be smaller than the horse? The laws of physics, baby."

"Libby…" Now her sister sounded exasperated, staring out across the creek. "It's *magic*."

"Oh." Elizabeth dropped a kiss on the top of her head. "Okay," she said, neither agreeing nor denying anything her sister said. "Come on. Let's go back before whoever he is gets tired of waiting, and leaves us here."

The self-appointed guardian was pacing back and

forth when they got back, not worried so much as…
alert. Elizabeth had a sudden flash of a stallion, proud
and wild, standing on a cliff, looking out across the
plains, then the image was gone, and it was just the
three of them, surrounded by pine trees and danger.
He gave them a once-over, and nodded. "This way."

There was no conversation as they walked, accompanied by the early morning sounds of birds and other
small animals. Maggie was good and kept her attention focused on where they were going, so not a single
creature kept them company—at least, not obviously.
The daylight grew brighter, and Elizabeth felt more and
more aware of the fact that she had slept in her clothing. There were pine needles in her socks and down the
back of her shirt, and her jacket was still damp from
the dew, and she just felt unbelievably grimy and wrin-
kled. At this point, she would trade all the sleep she had
managed last night, even with the good dreams, for ten
minutes under a hot shower.

Soon they heard the distant whoosh of cars passing by, and an airplane flying overhead, breaking into
the peaceful silence of the reserve. Elizabeth felt her
body tense at the reminders of civilization, and then
the trees thinned, and they came to a high wire fence,
blocking them in.

It was twice the height of the fence they had gone
over on the other side of the forest, and there were jagged curls of barbed wire on the top. How were they
supposed to get over that?

"This way," the man said, gesturing to a small slice in the fence.

Elizabeth wondered how their guide knew about it, or if he had made it himself, but thought better of asking.

"They should repair that," Maggie said primly, even as she was slipping through, her bag held low to fit through. Elizabeth went next, and then their guide followed, having to maneuver his broader frame carefully to avoid being snagged on the wires. The fence was at the top of a small grassy rise alongside a paved two-lane road, lined at intervals with telephone poles.

"This is the county road," he said. "There's a town about a mile or so down that way."

"Thank you,' Elizabeth said again, and suddenly remembered her manners. "I'm sorry, we never formally introduced ourselves. I'm Elizabeth. This is Margaret." She didn't give their last names, just in case.

"Good luck" was all he said in return, and then turned and went back through the fence, and disappeared into the woods.

"Wow," Maggie said, watching him go with a disappointed look on her face. "I really liked him better as a unicorn."

Chapter 4

While the girls were traveling south through the woods, they were the subject of a heated discussion back in the Community, where the Elders had gathered for an emergency meeting.

"What do you mean, you're not doing anything?" A man's voice, high-pitched and showing annoyance, filled the meeting room, demanding an answer.

"That is not what he said, Alan," another man said, but his expression was one of annoyance, as well. "Ray, don't you think…"

"I share your concern, everyone." The voice was smooth and practiced, without being too polished, and matched the man speaking. He was tall and solid, dressed, like the others, in jeans and shirt, both well-worn. Standing at the head of the long, wood-paneled room, his gaze met theirs evenly, squarely, and his shoulders were open even as his hands moved as he spoke. "Alan, Mark is correct, that was not what I said. Everyone, please believe me when I say that I too am concerned. Those poor girls, the past year has been so difficult for them, first losing their parents and then, well, poor Maggie just hasn't been the same since then, has she?"

The others in the room nodded, sobered by the reminder of those who were lost to the flu epidemic the year before. Every member of the Community had lost a loved one, it seemed, but some were harder struck. The survivors—younger, stronger children like Maggie—still bore evidence of their illness, in their lungs and their limbs.

Ray nodded as well, his body language perfectly echoing their own sorrow. "And in times of stress, we often act out of character. Elizabeth should have come to us first, of course, but she is a sensible girl—" all of eleven years younger than he, but decades younger than most of the others in the room "—and she will take good care of her sister, I am sure of that. And that is why I am not convinced that we need to *do* anything, specifically, to bring them back, or otherwise interfere with their lives.

"However, because it is…a world full of dangers, I've sent Jordan to find her, and keep an eye on them, make sure that they don't get into too much trouble."

That seemed to satisfy most of his inquisitors, but one woman refused to be consoled.

"But why did they leave? And to abandon everything, for Libby to just leave the bakery like that..." Judy sounded as though she was near to tears. "It's so unlike her!"

Ray leaned forward, catching her gaze and holding it like a snake charmer might his snake. "Oh, Judy, you know that sometimes we need a little distance, to understand what things close to us truly mean. It's how we learn, how we grow."

Ray had a soothing voice and a calming conviction that seemed to melt worries away, without dismissing the fears as foolish or unworthy, and Judy was no exception. Her expression visibly smoothed out and calmed down, and she patted her husband's arm as though he had been the one who was upset. "That's true. We forget...we came to the Community as adults, but the girls were born here, and it's all they've ever known. Even the Amish go away when they're teenagers, to see the outside world before they make their final choice, and we can't claim to be more reclusive than they are!"

There was some muted laughter from the others in the room, seven total. His fellow Elders had come to him that morning, worried about the seeming disappearance of two of their younger members, so suddenly. Judy and her husband, Mark, were personal friends of the Sweets; he suspected that they had pushed the others into speaking up and forcing a meeting.

Thankfully, he had received word of the girls' departure before anyone else, and had been ready for the appearance of his fellow Elders and neighbors, an answer smooth on his tongue.

"It was an impulsive move on their part, clearly, to not tell anyone, to simply up and leave. But their belongings are still here, they did not transfer the title to their house." No need to tell anyone about the recipes and deed to the bakery his men had retrieved, before the new owners could discover it. "They will be back, I assure you."

"Yes, but…" Stephan, the newest member of the Elders, elected to fill Ray's place when he was elevated, frowned in concern.

"I have asked Jordan to watch over them until they do return," Ray said, giving his final spin on the situation. Jordan was highly regarded in the Community; a seventh-grade math teacher, he had been born in the Community, which was important even to people who said it didn't matter. Ray bit back the rush of anger he still felt over that, and smiled gently instead, feeling his mouth strain at the effort. "He has orders to clear their path and give them time to do whatever it is they felt the need to do—see old friends of their parents, perhaps, or visit Disney World, whatever it is that young girls do. And then he will make sure they come home safely."

In fact, Jordan was under orders to bring them home, period. No matter what means were needed. Ray had plans for the Community, plans that were years in the making, and that required little Ms. Maggie to be home, safe and under his control.

She was the reason the Community existed, even if none of them realized it, yet.

"I wish they'd told me," another man said wistfully. "I've never been to Disney World, either. I'd have gone with them!"

Ray smiled as the others laughed again, but his hand, held out of sight at his waist, clenched. Andrew, the speaker, had been one of the few to object to his selection as the Old Lady's successor, had raised questions about someone not born in the Community leading it. Andrew and Sean Sweet, and their allies… There were too many people who questioned him.

The vote had gone his way, and he had confirmed his position formally, but Ray never forgot a challenge… or a challenger. Especially a man like Andrew, whose grandfather had been one of the original Founders, along with old Cab Sweet. Such a man was either useful—or dangerous. Ray hadn't decided where Andrew fell in the scheme of things yet.

Useful, he would be used. Dangerous…he would be removed. By force, if illness or accident did not take care of it for him.

But for now Andrew was in the undecided camp, and so it was still time for Ray to use the velvet glove, soothe his opponents into thinking they would get their way.

"Maggie and Elizabeth are our friends, our neighbors, our family. That allows us the right to worry, and to watch over them. But the genesis of the Community was in self-removal from the world, not forced removal."

The other Elders nodded at that.

"The girls will be back. They know where their home is. We simply need to trust them…and be ready with assistance, should they require it. And, of course, to welcome them home with our love, our compassion and our understanding, when they return."

It was a pretty speech, one he had rehearsed that morning, and it worked. Most of them, reassured, left the meeting room, heading back to their daily chores and lives. They might be the Elders, but they were just as happy to let him handle everything, in the day-to-day running of the Community. After all, if it was important it would come to a vote, right?

Ray was about to relax when he realized that, in addition to himself and his assistant, Glen, Judy's husband had remained behind.

"Yes, Mark?" Ray looked expectantly at the older man. Most matters were raised in public, in the weekly meeting, so this had to be something Mark wanted to keep private, away even from his own wife.

"I'm curious why you sent Jordan. He's our best negotiator, and the Dantern buyer is supposed to be here tomorrow, to price the wool. We needed him here."

Ah. The Community tried to be self-reliant, selling or bartering within their members to handle most daily needs, but many of the crafters sold their wares to the outside world, as well. Dantern was a nationwide shop that had a yearly contract with the small farm outside town. As Judy had said, they might have removed themselves from the daily technological impositions of television, internet and other forms of mass media, but they were still part of the larger world. Mark was one of their best businessmen, but he would not want anyone—especially his wife—to see him putting money before people. This was easily dealt with.

"Jordan knows Elizabeth and Maggie, he was friends with their parents. He wanted to go." Ray made a gesture with his hands, the perfect image of a man who gave in to familial ties over commerce, but only reluctantly, and aware that it was foolishness. "Truthfully, I am hoping that he will be able to convince them to come home right away. Elizabeth is a grown woman, but Maggie… I don't like someone as delicate as she being out there with only her sister to protect her. I try not to be sexist, but…it's a cold place for two girls without experience or money."

Elizabeth had cash, of course. The bakery did a steady business both within the Community and outside, so there would have been easy access to cash in the till—but they had no credit cards, no ATM cards. If they ran out of money, they would be dependent upon strangers, and Elizabeth was far too practical a girl to trust someone she didn't know.

Then again, he had thought she was too practical a girl to run, too. He had misjudged her, underestimated how spooked she had become, after the boy's unfortunate accident with the rope. He would not make that mistake that again.

"I hope that you're right," Mark said now. "I love the girls as though they were my own, but we have an obligation to keep everyone else running smoothly, too."

"Indeed, I couldn't agree more," Ray said, taking the older man's arm and walking with him toward the door. "The Community has been self-supporting for almost fifty years now, and I don't want a thing to change, I assure you."

The door closed behind Mark, and Ray turned to look back at the man remaining. Glen's cool gaze met his evenly.

"No, indeed," Ray said. "I don't want a thing to change…yet."

Chapter 5

It took Josh all of ten minutes, heading back to the campsite where he'd let his charges sleep, to start wondering how long it would take those men to find the girls again. The search had been called off, yes, but why, and for how long? He still didn't know why those men had wanted to take them—maybe they were escaped mental patients, and those were doctors or orderlies come to retrieve them?

He discarded the thought as soon as it appeared. Maggie was a little odd, perhaps, but they were both as sane as he—maybe more so, he thought ruefully, feeling the burn of the rut start again, just under his skin.

So why had the search been called off, when they were almost within range? If they knew the girls were in here… Were they even now blanketing the area, waiting? Their leader didn't seem to be the sort to give up, and he would probably be holding a grudge. Who was he to them? Not father, and not brother… Could he possibly be Elizabeth's lover? Any lover who treated a woman like that would be ex-lover in a heartbeat, and rightfully so. An ex-lover, then? If so, Josh wished he'd kicked the guy harder.

"Not your problem, Mustang," he told himself. "You need to get home, and deal with this rut once and for all, and get your life back in line, not caretake two complete strangers."

The rut was inevitable, undeniable and a pain in the… He swore, and adjusted his jeans for comfort as he walked. A pain in the everywhere. The itch to shift was shivering over his skin, coaxing him into taking his four-legged form again. Another time and place he might have given in, but not here. Not now. In that form he thought with his instincts more than his brain, and the rut made that—made *him*—too dangerous, especially out here, surrounded by strangers.

The itch didn't care, crawling around inside him like an entire farm of fire ants. To distract himself, he kept thinking about Elizabeth and Maggie. He wondered how much cash the girls had on them, if any—they had been dressed well, but not that well, and their backpacks were hardly stuffed with bills…and did they know enough not to use credit cards, so they couldn't be traced? Did they have a plan, someone they were running to, rather than simply running away?

Not your problem, he reminded himself, kicking apart the branches that had been their bedding, and moving on to where he had left his pack. It was still there, as expected. Not that he had much—a bachelor stallion traveled light, and when the rut had summoned him, a few changes of clothes had seemed enough weight to bear. He regretted the books and knickknacks he had left behind; hopefully he would be able to reclaim them from storage when he was done.

Or, he wouldn't be worrying about them at all if the rut wasn't dealt with, soon. Days, he estimated.

No, Maggie and Libby were not his problem anymore; he had his own crap to deal with, and the clock, as the clichés went, was ticking. He had waited too long already.

Mustang had been minding his own business up until fourteen days ago, working on a fishing boat, the sea air as unlike his home as possible, when the need hit him. He woke in his bunk, sweating, a hard-on that could break cement pulsing between his legs, the sound of feminine laughter echoing through his dreams, and dread in his stomach.

Rut. Every member—every male member—of the herd went through it. But you never quite believed it was going to get you, until it did.

He had finished out his contract, and when the boat docked, tossed his belongings into storage and set out for home. It was purely bad luck that found him within Maggie's reach; the itch to change had gotten so bad the night before, he'd been afraid he would make the shift in his sleep. The thought of waking in a motel room, the bed broken around his hooves, was not a pleasant one. He'd chosen to sleep outside, rather than risk that and the inevitable discovery. Because of that choice, he had, apparently, been within calling distance.

Maggie. Sweet, tired-looking Maggie. And Elizabeth—he preferred that to the earlier Libby—of the long legs and the firm hands. They were on the run— why? Because of Maggie, he guessed. Magical Maggie. The danger came from those men? From whoever sent those men? Either way, there was little chance they could escape, not without help.

He hoped they had help, somewhere.

The thought stayed with him, no matter how much he tried to dislodge it. Barely an hour later he stopped in his tracks, blew out an exasperated sigh and turned around, heading…not west, the way his rut was telling him to go, not back toward home, but south into town, after his runaways.

The need to go home, the urge to find an appropriate mate along the way, could wait a little while longer. At least long enough to make sure that Elizabeth and Maggie were safe.

"Baby, stay here, all right?"

"I'm not a baby," Maggie said, but it was an automatic objection. Elizabeth would be calling her that when they were both ancient. "And yes, I'll stay right here—" and she stamped the pavement with her sneakered foot in emphasis "—until you give me the all clear or a truck barrels down like it's gonna hit me. Or a forest fire blazes at me. Or a bear..."

"All right, all right, I get it. You're smart enough to stay out of trouble. Sit."

Maggie sat, clearly pleased at having made her sister smile, despite their worries.

They had walked several miles down that county road into Patsmilling, a small, traditional-looking New England town, and found the local police station without too much trouble. It was on the aptly named Front Street, across from the post office and town hall, and down the street from the two-engine fire department.

Elizabeth looked up and down the street, her heart beating faster than it should have. There were a few people out, running errands or heading back to work, but nobody was looking at them, nobody pointing or making furtive cell-phone calls. The police station didn't look very impressive: a two-story redbrick building with a small wooden sign outside that identified it, and two squad cars parked at the curb outside. Still, they didn't have to be an armed fortress to do their job: anything larger than a break-in or vandalism case, and the cops probably relied on the county to handle it, but Patsmilling looked and sounded sleepy enough that it was likely they didn't have anything larger very often....

"Libby?"

The one word in her sister's voice said, clearly, *Why are you standing there? Why haven't you gone in yet? Is something wrong?*

Elizabeth risked looking over her shoulder. Maggie was sitting, as she had promised, on the bench outside the post office. One woman was forgettable. Two females, obviously sisters…someone might remember that. Maggie should be perfectly safe here, in full view of government employees, right? There wasn't anything to stop Elizabeth from going inside and asking for help Nothing excerpt her own nerves and uncertainty, anyway.

Maggie talked to animals. Elizabeth dreamed. Unlike her sister's ability, Elizabeth didn't put much stock into her dreams. Yes, they told her things that were going to happen, or might happen, but dreams were tricky things and she wasn't comfortable trusting them. And this wasn't even a dream, just a feeling that going into that building would be a very bad idea. Involving the police had not been her original plan. She had no proof to give them, only fear and coincidence, and she was terrified that they would think that she was the crazy one, unfit to care for Maggie.

But what were their options? Ray, and maybe all of the Elders, wanted Maggie back at the Community, and were willing to snatch her in a public place to accomplish that. Elizabeth had cash, but not an endless amount, and no way to access their bank account without Ray using that to track them down—the Community didn't rely on computers and such, but that didn't mean they couldn't and wouldn't use them when needed. And just running as fast as they could wasn't an option anymore, not with Jordan and his goons so close on their heels—he shouldn't have been able to find them so easily, but he had. Why should she assume tomorrow would be any different? Anywhere they went, he could find them.

They needed something official standing between them—someone with the ability to hold Jordan off, make life uncomfortable for the Community if she and Maggie weren't left alone. Her instinct, honed by Community tradition, was to never involve outsiders…but she was about to become an outsider herself. So it made sense, didn't it?

Yes. This was a smart move. Three generations of good public relations, being known as "that little village of the folk who live off the grid but don't make trouble," would be gone if the media picked up a "runaway returned against her wishes" story. No matter how much they wanted Maggie back, the Elders would never let Ray cause that sort of trouble. Once she walked into the police station, she and Maggie would be safe.

Still, she stood there, aware of how rumpled and tired she looked, and couldn't seem to make her feet move.

"You're getting a bad feeling, aren't you?" Her sister's voice was small and worried, and something inside her shriveled at the sound.

"No. It's all right, Maggie."

She forced herself to take a step, then another. Not for herself. For Maggie. Maggie could not go back to the Community. Maggie could never go back there....

She heard Maggie give a chirp, and then an answering chirp from one of the trees that lined the street. Even in plain sight, her sister couldn't help herself; she would call the birds to her. It was okay. So long as she didn't call an eagle or a bear, or...

"Stop thinking. Keep walking."

Another step, and her feet locked, still on the sidewalk, in the shadows of the post office. A car pulled down the street, and parked on the curb, just behind the second cop car. A man got out, and Elizabeth felt her breath catch in her throat, and a wave of betrayal flooded her.

Mark. An Elder, a man who had been friends with her parents, a man she had thought untouched by Ray's schemes... He might be there to find them on his own, he might have been worried enough about them to leave town and come here...but how had he known to come here? Who had sent him, and why? How had they *known?*

He stopped, as though hearing her thoughts, and looked up and down the street, thankfully on his own side, before continuing into the police station.

Panic took over, and she turned and strode back to the bench, catching Maggie's hand in her own, practically dragging her sister off the wooden bench and scattering the handful of sparrows that were eating crumbs from her pocket.

"Libby?" Her sister's voice was hushed, not carrying beyond the two of them. Scared, and uncertain. She sounded like she was on the edge of tears.

Elizabeth felt the same way.

"We have to go. Now."

They walked along the sidewalk, keeping their heads down, moving past the occasional pedestrian, trying to look as casual as strangers in a small town could. They had to get out of there, had to leave town. If Mark was there, there might be others, and if so where were they? Her thoughts fluttered like startled pigeons, and her feet took her down a side street without her having made a conscious decision to turn. There was a wide alley off to the right and, following that same instinct, Elizabeth tugged Maggie into it without looking, only to give a gasp of surprise when a pair of strong arms caught her by the shoulders.

"What's wrong?"

A voice, recently familiar, came with the touch, and her panic died down even as her heart rate sped up at the contact. His hands were just as firm and strong as Jordan's, but the feeling they inspired was completely and totally different. Instead of fear and rage, she felt calmness and strength, energy surging inside her, as though she had a host of angels at her back.

"You came back," Maggie crowed, then quieted with

a nervous look over her shoulder, but nobody raced down the street and into their alleyway after them.

"What's wrong?" their rescuer asked again, more urgently this time.

Elizabeth felt the words flow out of her. "Someone… someone we know, just went into the police station. He might be…but I don't know. I can't risk it."

Incoherent, but he seemed to understand. His hands let go of her shoulder, and instead one arm slid around her waist, while his other hand took up Maggie's. "They're going to be looking for two girls," he said.

"Or two girls and a horse," Maggie said, and when he glared at her she just smiled impishly. As far as she was concerned, her expression said, her sister and her unicorn could take care of anything.

"They're looking for two females," he said again. "Three people they might not see. They're not expecting to see you with a male."

Elizabeth flinched, the memory of the last male she had trusted still hot and fierce in her memory, the first sight of Cody's body as they lowered him to the ground, the soft murmur of talk that cut off as she cried his name, the hands holding her back, keeping her from him…

The stranger kept talking, and she hoped neither he nor Maggie had noticed her momentary distress. "Even with me you're noticeable right now. We need to get you out of those clothes, and dump the bags, and change your looks."

"We need to get out of sight," Elizabeth agreed, forcing the memories back to deal with the present. "But it's too far back to the forest, and—"

"There is a motel at the edge of town," he interrupted. "We can get a room there, figure out what we're going to do next."

Elizabeth heard the "we" and blinked; "we" sounded like more than a stroll out of town, but she was in no position to argue or question. Her instincts had been right to keep herself out of the police station, and had taken her to where he was waiting, and now they were telling her to go with this man. So she went, intensely aware of the warm arm around her waist, and the equally warm body pressed against hers, tall and sturdy and smelling unlike anything else she'd ever smelled—like some potent combination of clean sweat and the best aftershave and sunshine on grass. The smell caught in her nostrils, and made her want to turn and nuzzle into him, like a kitten kneading a freshly laundered blanket. Whatever else he might be, she was definitely responding to him as a male—a *human* male.

Stupid, stupid. Understandable—a friendly voice when she desperately needed one—but still stupid.

She had told him the truth, she wasn't a virgin—there had been Michael back in high school, and then Drew, whom she'd loved but, in the end, not liked very much, but neither of them had ever made her feel like this, just from a touch of skin-to-skin, however innocently. Neither of them had ever made her feel both protected and strong at the same time, like she could tangle with anything, and win. Her knight-errant…knight and horse in one, just like a chess piece.

And he hadn't shown even the slightest interest in her, that way.

Elizabeth leaned against him, and told herself it was just part of the act, showing the rest of the world a happy family unit, nothing unusual here, nothing to see, move along, no girl with unusual talents, no man who might or might not change shape, no woman trying to hide from her lifelong family because she was suddenly terrified of them…no, nothing at all unusual here.

For a moment, walking in step with a man whose name she didn't even know—she believed it.

The motel was everything the town would suggest: small, slightly run-down, but reasonably clean and in-expensive. Their guardian went into the small white of-fice and made the arrangements. When he came out, he had a single key on a plastic tag in his hand.

"I only had enough cash for one room," he said, apol-ogetically, pushing the shank of blond hair off his fore-head as though embarrassed. "They don't take credit cards for a one-night stay."

Elizabeth gave a helpless shrug. She was in no posi-tion to play diva right then—and they had already spent the night together, after all, however bizarrely. "I prom-ise not to take advantage of you," she said, meaning to make light of the situation, but when he looked at her, something in his gaze made the words dry up in her mouth. Those dark eyes were filled with an intense hunger and need and a heat that bypassed her brain entirely and went like a lightning strike into her chest, spreading heat and sizzle all the way to her knees.

Oh. Maybe she wasn't alone, feeling the way she felt? She blinked, her gaze locked on his, until he swore under his breath, barely loud enough to hear, and broke the connection by looking away.

Freed, she could breathe again, but her only thought had been the desire to take his face in her hands, turn his chin so that she could see those eyes again and figure out if that look had been meant for her personally, or if he just needed to get laid, and never mind that the last thing she needed was a quick hot anything. She wanted that look to have been for *her*.

But he refused to look at her, the muscle in his neck cording with the strain of keeping his head turned away, and he stared into the parking lot at the row of white doors. She didn't know how to force the issue, or even if she should.

Maggie, heedless of the tension quivering between the two of them, grabbed at the key and started down the row of rooms, counting off numbers.

Their room was at the far end of the row, number seventeen.

The moment the key turned in the lock, Maggie made a mad rush for the bathroom, closing the door with a definite snick, and they heard the water turn on almost immediately, followed by the sound of the toilet flushing.

"She's…not used to roughing it," Elizabeth said, almost apologetically, uncertain how to react. Would he just look at her? Or did she really want him to? The flutters in her chest could go either way.

"And you are?" He looked at her then, and his eyes were hooded, bland, telling her nothing and making her wonder if she had imagined the earlier heat. Then he took her hand in his own, turning it over and looking at it carefully. She shivered at the feel of that touch, but forced herself to show no other reaction. That flash of heat and longing had been so fast, so unexpected, and gone so quickly, she might have imagined it. *Stress,* she told herself. *Stress and loss and you're lucky you're still standing right now.* Although if he didn't stop holding her hands like that, his fingers sliding up and down her palm, she wasn't sure how much longer she *would* be standing.

"Strong hands," he said, almost conversationally. "Calloused but cared for. Nails neatly trimmed, no polish, cuticles groomed—you don't bite your nails. You work with your hands, but not outside. Not roughing it, no, but not afraid of hard work."

He suddenly seemed to realize what he was doing and let go of her, moving away. "You should use the shower next," he said. "I don't know how long we'll be able to stay here. I'm going to go out and pick up some things. Lock the door behind me, and yes, I know you knew to do that already, humor me, all right?"

He slipped out the door like a man escaping a firing squad, and Elizabeth wasn't sure if she should be insulted or amused. She locked the door and then, after a moment's thought, went to make sure that the single window locked as well, before drawing the shades closed. Then she went to roust her sister out of the bathroom, already imagining the feel of hot water against her skin.

Or maybe she'd turn it to cold, after all.

Chapter 6

When Elizabeth came out of the bathroom half an hour later, dressed again in her old jeans and a fresh T-shirt she pulled from her knapsack, he was back, and Maggie was trying on a brand-new windbreaker in dark blue. The bed was strewn with plastic bags with the logo of a chain store on them, one she remembered seeing as they walked into town, and he pointed to the smaller pile. "I wasn't sure what sizes you wore, so I improvised."

She put the thin towel she had been drying her hair with over the back of the single chair in the room, and went to investigate. The bags contained a couple of pullover tops in dark colors, and a pair of sweatpants, also dark, plus socks and a three-pack of cotton underwear, all in medium.

"Good guess," she said dryly. Large, she would have been offended, and small was always risky. Still, she appreciated the effort it had probably taken for him to choose the items at all. "Thank you."

He shrugged, still not looking at her. "They'll have description of your clothing. I figured the more we changed, the better. And I didn't know how many changes of underwear you'd stuffed in your bag."

Two, in point of fact. She'd hoped to be somewhere with a Laundromat by then. Maybe not.

"Thank you," she said again. She would repay him, somehow. Eventually. The feeling of being in debt was uncomfortable.

There was no windbreaker for her, but a heavy hooded sweatshirt. She pulled it on over her tank, and tested the length of the sleeves. A little long, but it worked.

"Libby, look!" Maggie pointed to the label on the hoodie. "A unicorn!"

Their companion winced; clearly he hadn't noticed the logo.

"It's okay," Maggie said in response to his wince. "Unicorns protect girls, right? That's why you're here." She nodded with absolute confidence.

"Right," Elizabeth said, unable to help herself. "Young girls with garlands in their hair and horns resting in their laps, everyone knows that."

She winced the moment she heard the double entendre, but he seemed to find that amusing, the way his narrow lips twitched and his dark eyes crinkled, as though suppressing a smile. And that look, that hot, heavy, considering look, was back in his gaze.

"If I put my horn into your lap…" he began, and Elizabeth narrowed her eyes at him, reminding him that Maggie was in the room, and too young for ribald comments, even if he were joking.

She was pretty sure that he was joking. And if he wasn't…what would she do then? That instant of heat between them… Elizabeth tried to dredge up some measure of concern, some worry at being in a motel room with a strange man, and couldn't. It wasn't simply that Maggie was there to play chaperone. Even after that look in his eyes, her every instinct told her that she had nothing to fear from him. Not physically, anyway. And even if he tried to play on her gratitude for rescuing them, Maggie was in the room with them.

She was honest enough with herself to admit to feeling a little bit of disappointment about that.

Maggie, ignoring their byplay, had tired of looking through her new clothing, and was busy taking everything out of her knapsack and putting it into the new carryall; like her clothing, it was similar to the one she had carried, only in a darker color.

"Bright colors attract attention?" Elizabeth asked quietly.

"Exactly."

His terse response annoyed her. "So does saying

'hey, you' all the time. You know our names, but we don't know yours."

He sat down on the edge of the bed, watching Maggie pack her things away, and didn't say anything.

"Hello?" she prompted him.

Maggie stopped and looked up at him as well, her face brightly expectant.

"Josh. Joshua Mustang."

Mustang? She started to make a joke, but the look on his face suggested that he'd probably heard them before. "Hello, Josh," she said, trying the name out on her tongue.

"Hello, Elizabeth."

"Libby," Maggie said, correcting him. "Her name's Libby."

He considered her then, studying her from toe to top with a quiet, somehow totally inoffensive stare that was as far from his earlier look as possible, but still carried enough weight to make anticipation curl in her stomach. "No," he said finally. "Elizabeth."

There really wasn't anything to say to that, so Elizabeth took her clothes from the pile on the bed and went back into the bathroom to change out of clothing that suddenly felt too grubby to be worn. When she came out again, now dressed in fresh underwear and the sweatpants, Maggie's new backpack was closed up and waiting by the door, and her sister was sound asleep curled up in the middle of the bed, next to where Josh was sitting.

"She just crawled up there and…out like a light." He sounded bemused at her utter confidence in him, but not surprised.

"I guess she thinks that unicorns are magically good."

"You don't?" His mood totally turned around, he feigned hurt, placing a hand against his heart as though she had stabbed him.

She went with the change, falling easily into repartee. "You may be good, but I'm not sure that you're magically *good*."

He laughed at that, and Maggie stirred, but didn't wake up.

Miss Elizabeth didn't know how right she was, he thought, studying her in her new clothing, standing there across the motel room like a challenge. The long dark hair was even darker when damp, and it fell all the way down her back like a horse's tail, but silken like… His imagination failed him. He had never seen anything so soft. His palm itched to touch it, to knot it up in his fist and…

The image of the first time he had seen her, just the day before, her hair being used as a rope to keep her from going to her sister's aid, struck him like a slap and he recoiled.

"There's a pair of scissors in that bag," he said, his voice gruff as he tried to erase that memory. "Do you want to do it, or should I?"

"Do what?"

"Cut your hair. Don't give me that look. It's too damn recognizable, and it's too damn easy to get snagged on something if you're trying to run."

He had been bumming around the country since he had been kicked out of the herd at nineteen, caring only for himself, and had no problems with being selfish and arrogant, among other things. He understood that about himself, made no apologies. But the look in her eyes when he told her to cut her hair… It made him feel like a total shit.

She had beautiful hair. She probably normally brushed it a hundred times every night, or something. Naked, draped in that shining curtain…

He couldn't even blame the rut for the way he hardened at that mental image. There wasn't a male alive and intact who wouldn't sweat to have that under him. Over him. Josh almost groaned out loud at the thought of her riding him for true, her hair falling over them both, sweat gleaming on her dusky skin, the press of flesh against flesh where their bodies joined….

His mouth went dry and his fingers clenched into his palm with desire, his cock painfully hard, pressing against the seam of his jeans. Where the hell had his control gone?

Rut. It was making him near-crazy. That was all.

Elizabeth picked up the scissors and looked at them doubtfully. They were good scissors, hair-cutting shears he'd had to look for, and pay extra for. He wouldn't ask her to do it with a cheap pair.

The look in her eyes was haunted, almost mourning, and he hated himself for asking in the first place, even with the most expensive shears, even if he could take her to the best salon in the country. He had to ask, though—and he had to insist. Every instinct in him warned that her hair was a weakness she couldn't afford. Either cut it or dye it; just shoving it under a cap wouldn't work, it was too easy for a hat to be dislodged, and the thought of someone else using it to restrain or hurt her made a rage rise in him that overrode even the fire-hot itch of the rut.

She worked the shears a few times, testing their balance. "My mother used to brush my hair out every morning. We'd sit on the porch, and she'd drink her coffee, and we'd listen to the sounds of the morning—people going to work, walking their dogs, the birds in the trees, and she'd brush it, a dozen strokes, crown to ends, until there wasn't a single knot or tangle."

Josh felt a cold shaft of guilt hit him, right in the gut. "All right, this was a bad idea, we'll find another way." Maybe they could dye it blue, make it so outlandish people would see it, and not the face below.

"No. No, you're right." Elizabeth's voice was low, but determined. "Everyone back home, anyone who might be looking for us, they know my hair. They'd never believe I'd cut it short. But...can we leave Maggie's hair long?"

"Yeah. We can leave Maggie's hair long." Hating himself, unable to stop, he moved across the room, taking the shears from her hands. "Sit down."

He moved the single chair in the room away from the mirror, so she didn't have to watch, and she sat, obediently, if reluctantly. Her hair was still damp from the shower, and smelled like shampoo and the last remnant of pine from her bed the night before. He had stood over them the hours they slept, keeping guard the way a stallion would over his herd, and the irony of it did not escape him.

He was a Mustang. It was more than an ironic family name: it was what he *was*, in his four-legged form. The rut pushing him to find a mate was part and parcel of his heritage, the same as his shape-shifting, and as impossible to ignore. His time as a bachelor stallion was over. It was the season for him to settle down and start a family of his own, and not roam aimlessly anymore. But the rules were blunt: he needed a virgin. Elizabeth was smart, and brave, and the depth of feeling she had for her sister, the patience and caring, impressed him as much as her beauty and strength turned him on. He would take her to bed with pleasure, and give her as much pleasure as he could, in return, but this woman was not for him—and he was not for her. Not long-term.

All he could do was make sure that she and her sister were safe.

Lifting a length of her shining black hair in his hand, the damp strands clinging to his skin as though protesting his actions, he used the shears quickly, trying not to think about what he was doing. The strands fell to the floor, scattering against the pale carpet, until there was more on the ground than left on her head. The ends, rather than touching her waist, now danced just above her shoulders, and even under the crap motel lights the sheen reminded him of blackbirds flying overhead, their glossy feathers glinting in the sunlight.

"It's not stylish, but you can get it trimmed once you're safe," he said gruffly.

Elizabeth's hand rose to touch the ragged ends, and her head tilted from side to side, testing the new weight.

"I feel five pounds lighter," she said, her tone wondering. "It's…weird. My neck is cold." She hesitated, then stood up, going to the mirror to examine her new look.

While she was occupied, Josh took a lock of the shorn hair and, not stopping to question why he was doing it, curled it into a coil and slipped it into the pocket of his jeans.

"Oh." She was primping in front of the mirror now, pulling the strands this way and that, trying to see how different styles might look. "I don't look like me anymore."

"That's the point," he agreed. Her cheekbones were even more prominent, and her eyes seemed larger, more intense. He suspected that, rather than making her inconspicuous, he had just made her more noticeable.

Hopefully, she would be fighting off would-be lovers, not…whomever she had been running from.

The thought of her being with someone else, some other man touching that hair, that skin, of some other man protecting her, some other man claiming her, made his fingers tighten around the handle of the scissors until his muscles cramped and protested. His control was totally shredded. The rut had control of his emotions; any and every female past puberty would become a trigger for him, soon, he suspected.

The legends said that he would know his mate when he saw her, that the bond would be immediate. Not all matches came from within the herd—new blood kept them healthy, vigorous. He had never wondered about that before, if a human mate would know him, too. If she would be able to accept him. What happened if she didn't?

All he knew was that she needed to be pure, a virgin. Almost impossible, in this world, and yet he had to believe she was out there for him. Somewhere.

The coil of hair in his pocket seemed to burn, he was so aware of it, mocking him. A memento of memories he would never have, when he was an old man with foals of his own running with the herd. Or…

He slammed the door on the other possibility, refusing to even consider it. She was out there. He knew it, in his gut.

Elizabeth was talking. "Thank you. For everything.

I don't understand why you're helping us, but...thank you."

He got a grip on his emotions, and forced a smile. "Well, your sister called me, didn't she?"

Her eyes looked at the carpet, where the remains of her hair were strewn. "You think we're crazy."

He let out a harsh bark of laughter, making her look up again, quickly. "Your sister thinks I'm a unicorn. That's pretty crazy, yeah."

"But she's right, isn't she? You were...you are."

He stared at her until she blinked and looked away, uncomfortable. "You accept that so easily, like it's nothing. Maybe to you it isn't—your sister talks to animals. Who the hell are you, Elizabeth?"

She ran a hand through the drying strands of her hair, and shrugged, a quick, jerky gesture as much of nerves as anything else. "Would it be very horrible if I said I didn't want to talk about myself? It's not you, it's just that Maggie and I, we need to disappear. If Jordan were to find you, afterward...the less you know about us, about where we're going, the better I'll feel."

He was almost insulted that she thought he would crack under some human's questioning, but he didn't push it. Maggie would tell him, if he asked.

"But you..." She sat in the chair and stared at him, her earlier indecision masked by renewed fascination. "A unicorn. Are there others? Can they all change shape? Are the legends true? Are..." She laughed, breathless. "I sound like Maggie, now. You asked how

I could accept it so easily. I'm not sure I can, that I have. It's against every law of nature or science I've ever learned, and you have to admit, it makes us both sound insane to even be talking about it."

Elizabeth ran both hands through her hair again, letting the strands flutter back down to caress her jawline. "But you were right. I…I have dreams, sometimes. Warnings. Might be coincidence, might be instinct, might be anything. But my sister is… Maggie is magical, in her own way. I've seen cougars come out of the mountains and sleep at her feet while she sang to them. I've seen a golden eagle land in front of her, and let her touch it, without fear or aggression. A man who changes into a horse is just the next step up from impossible." She stopped to consider that. "Okay, two steps up."

"I'm not a horse." That was, somehow, worse than being called an animal.

He shouldn't tell her anything. Shouldn't share any more than she had shared with him, and for the same reasons. But it was so rare to find someone he could actually talk to, without denying who or what he was, and the opportunity was too great to resist.

"We're not horses. But we're…not human, either. Not entirely." His voice fell, almost unconsciously, to the singsong tone the great-aunts used when they told the story to the yearlings.

"Long, long ago, more than a dozen generations ago, the herd came to this land, to the then-wild plains, looking for a place to run free. We built homes in our human forms, and ran with the wild horses in our four-legged forms, teaching our offspring how to live according to their nature, unafraid.

"The native tribes called us horse-brothers, and knew better than to try to rope us. We lived, if not in peace, then coexistence. When the white men came, our elders remembered the stories that had sent us here in the first place, and we hid ourselves from them, scattering the villages, destroying all traces of our world and hiding among mankind, living and breeding among them—but always longing for the freedom of the open range.

"Times changed. The cowboys were no friends of ours, then or now. We took the name Mustang to identify ourselves to each other, and show our sympathy for the wild horses and open spaces. And so it has been, ever since."

Where once the herd had numbered in the hundreds, roaming the land at will, there were only dozens now, broken into homes and jobs and human forms. Only twice a year did they gather together to roam the plains, to reform the bonds that held them together, and teach the yearlings what they were. He missed it, suddenly, with a longing that was even stronger than the rut, if carved from the same root.

Elizabeth looked at him, her dark eyes enthralled, her pink lips open just enough to let her tongue peek through, an unconscious gesture that made him want to reach out with a fingertip and stroke that tip until her mouth opened for him, and he could take possession of it, plunder the sweet depths until she moaned his name, her arms and legs opening to take him in....

"So you're saying that the legends of the shy, mystical unicorn are just so much bunk?"

He slapped the erotic image away, and tried to focus on what she was saying. "I don't know about the legends, where they came from or how much truth there is to them, or if maybe somewhere else there's another... branch of the family that might hew more closely to what the storybooks say."

The stories might have become legends, but Mustang were very much flesh and blood and instinct and animal needs. Females stayed close to their dams, usually settling in the same area, but males were kicked out after puberty hit, knocking around the world on their own, looking...for what, he still wasn't sure. The stallions who came back tended not to talk about what they'd done or seen, at least not to yearlings, and the ones who didn't come back...well, they weren't spoken of, either.

Instinct drove them, told them what to do. It sent them away from the older males for their own safety, and then forced them to abandon whatever life they'd had as a bachelor to return home, to find their mate.

The rut drove them like a spur, and, if his unwanted forays into erotic daydreams were any indication, resisting it led to violence, or madness. That fact he kept to himself. If she knew what he was going through, how close to the rutting edge he was, she'd probably grab

Maggie and run—right into the arms of the men she was running from.

Elizabeth was still caught up in the little he had told her, however. Her eyes practically sparkled with fascination. "And you can change shape? You move from one form to the other…like a werewolf?"

"Nothing at all like a wolf," he said, affronted. That was worse than being called a horse!

Her gaze darkened slightly. "I'm sorry, I'm just reaching… All I know are werewolves, and that makes more sense, physically, the body mass and musculature. That's the part I'm having trouble with. The change. It just doesn't seem possible. It's not scientifically possible."

Her voice was so filled with frustration, both at the impossibility and her inability to puzzle it out, that he couldn't stay annoyed. "It doesn't fit with the science we have in textbooks now, maybe. But that doesn't mean it's not actually possible." Suddenly exhausted, he sat on the desk opposite her, and studied her face carefully. The shorter hair was starting to curl a little, now that it was dry, and she brushed at it, self-conscious under his scrutiny. "What about magic?"

"Magic?" She shook her head. "There isn't any magic. It's… It can all be explained. Somehow."

"You can explain magic?" He leaned forward, curious. He had never really thought about what he did or how he did it; it simply *was,* like having a nose and toes.

"Not without a circular explanation of it being magic.

That's the point of magic." She frowned at him, indignant. "You're trying to confuse me."

He was. She was cute when she was confused, her eyes narrowing and her regal nose scrunched up. "Some things are just naturally confusing and therefore must be taken on faith."

"I'm not very good at faith. I never have been. I like evidence." She sounded regretful, and he wondered what in her past had been proven to her, so harshly.

"You need evidence. And then you'll believe?"

He didn't know why it was so important, why he needed to see her face when she saw him, really saw him in his primal form. But he did.

Without waiting for her response, he reached inside himself for that awareness that always lingered, the sense of self in another form. And that simply, that easily, he felt his skin soften and change, the shiver of the shift taking him from two-legged to four-legged self.

He had never shifted before in front of someone who didn't already know, who didn't understand, and he braced himself for whatever reaction she might have.

"Oh."

His perspective was different in his four-legged self; his eyes saw differently, he heard and smelled differently, and from a different angle. But he saw Elizabeth clearly, the wonder and awe in her eyes as she approached him. They were crowded in the motel room, caught between bed and desk and chair, and she was very close to him now, close enough that he could smell all the tiny threads of scent that made up the distinct awareness of "Elizabeth." She reached out, running her strong hand across his withers, down his back then back up to his neck. It was a caress; the kind a girl would give to a horse, but he felt it as a man would feel the touch of a woman, and his skin shuddered, the only way he could express what she was doing to him.

"Maggie was right, you are beautiful," she said. "That's just…amazing. You can hear me, understand me?"

He snorted, and she clearly heard the rebuke.

"All right, sorry. It's just…I'm taking a minute to deal with this, all right?" She moved around to stand in front of him, and he had to shift his head slightly to keep watching her, his range of vision in this form different from his human sight. Her hand reached up and, knowing what she wanted, his lowered his head slightly.

Her hand on his horn was possibly the most erotic thing he had ever felt. He felt the quiver from his hooves to his ears, and had to force himself to stay still, to not shift back to human form and take her then and there, and be damned the girl sleeping unawares not two feet away. Elizabeth didn't seem to notice, running her fingers lightly over the tapering length, then back down to the base, letting her fingers rest on the tangled blond forelock. "You probably should change back," she said regretfully. "Talk about not being conspicuous…"

The change back was just as swift, and Elizabeth found her fingers caught in his hair still when he shifted.

A blush stained her cheek, and she tried to move away, but he caught her hand in his and, gently, impulsively, dropped a soft kiss on the tips of her fingers before letting her go. It might have been the hardest thing he'd ever done, letting go of that work-strong hand.

"So." She sounded a little dazed, her eyes wide with what he suspected was more than unicorn-inspired shock or awe.

"So," he echoed, waiting to see what she would do, or say. Anyone else, he would have expected her to grab the still-sleeping Maggie and run like hell out the door, no matter what else was chasing her. Normal humans were, well, normal. He wasn't. But this was Elizabeth, who loved her sister who spoke to animals, and fought like a wild thing when captured, and let the shift happen in front of her without more than a startled gasp. Who touched him like the lover he could never let her become.

"That was…" She shook her head, and he heard the stress rising in her voice, and saw her tamp it back down again, not letting it diminish the wonder. "Either Ray was right and I'm insane, and you're just a hallucination, or you're a were-unicorn."

"You're not insane." She might be, of course. He had no idea who Ray was or why he might have said that, but he knew that she was as sane as…probably *more* sane than he was right now.

"So you're a were-unicorn. One of a pack of them, apparently, roaming the American West."

He was, absurdly, stung by the matter-of-fact amusement in her voice, even though he suspected much of it was aimed at herself, not him. "A herd, actually. And we don't roam, except during reunions. Most of us live in houses, with spouses and kids, and sometimes even a dog and a cat and a tank of tropical fish."

"And you aren't ruled by the phases of the moon."

He shook his head. "I am a vegetarian, though." He confessed that as though admitting to a terrible sin.

She laughed, a hiccupy sort of laugh, and shook her head, wiping the inside corner of her eye, as though a tear had started there. "Of course you are."

Elizabeth sat back on the edge of the desk, looking at Josh, really looking at him. He seemed content to let her do so, leaning against the wall with his arms relaxed at his sides, his head tilted and his gaze steady while he waited. She had never really considered blonds sexy before, and he wore his hair longer than she liked on men, down to the base of his neck, but when she looked at it she saw the flowing mane against a sleekly muscled neck, and felt the touch of it under her fingertips as he carried them to safety, and she allowed as how, on him, the long hair was a good look.

She also remembered how wide and solid his chest was, and how strong his arms had been around her waist when they walked out of town, and her gaze dropped to the long legs hidden under worn denim, and wondered if they were as sleekly muscled as the unicorn's, and if it was true what they said about stallions…and if that carried over to the human form.

Oh. A blush flushed her cheeks and made her want to fan herself to cool down. Bad thoughts. Worse: useless thoughts. His earlier question about her virginity had clearly showed her that much of the legend, at least, was true—a unicorn bonded to a virgin, not a woman who had been sexually active. She shrugged, mentally, trying to tell herself it didn't hurt, it didn't matter. He was here for Maggie, not her. And that was fine, so long as Maggie was protected. She could take care of herself, so long as he took care of her sister's safety.

"You can't go to the cops now," he said, switching gears fast enough to make her dizzy. "Not if you think whoever's chasing you has gotten to them first. I can only imagine the story they're spinning—kidnapping, at best."

Her mouth went dry. "You think he would do that?" When she had walked away from the police station, she had only considered the immediate risk of discovery, not that Ray would actively set the police on her, the way she'd been planning to use them, or worse. "No. No, he wouldn't. He can't. If the police get involved… That was why I was going to them in the first place. Ray can't risk publicity, or the rest of the Elders will force him to step down for the good of the Community. We don't have television or internet, but the news gets to us anyway, and someone would hear and start to ask questions. He can't afford questions. Not yet."

She wasn't sure what Ray had planned, only that it involved her sister, and the Community, and that while there were a lot of people there who thought he could do no wrong, he didn't have everyone in his pocket just yet, and so still had to move carefully. If he were confident of his hold on the town, she and Maggie would never have gotten beyond the town limits; there would have been no polite summons, but a knock on the door and a quiet exit, Maggie in one direction and Elizabeth…

She didn't know what he would do with her. To her. He wouldn't dare hurt her, not if he wanted Maggie to behave, but that didn't mean she would be safe, either.

It had to be Maggie's ability that he wanted, he had to have found out somehow, someone saying something while they were sick with the flu, feverish and rambling…but when she tried to understand what he might want her little sister to do, she came up against a blank wall. Calling birds? Playing with deer, and soothing the occasional black bear? A zookeeper would find it useful, but her imagination failed her as to what use it could be put to other than that. Maggie's ability was amazing, but it was limited, and the family had always been so careful to teach her that it was wrong to "call" someone or something against their will. That was why she had apologized to Josh. Calling people—even four-legged people—was wrong. Maggie would never do anything like that.…

Unless it was to protect her older sister.

But no matter how she tried, Elizabeth could not imagine how Maggie's ability could be misused.

"I hope that you're right," Josh said, and she was startled for a moment before realizing that he was replying to what she had said before, not what she was thinking. "Do you have a fallback plan?" he asked. "Once you had alerted the cops that someone was after you, what had you intended to do then?"

She did have a backup plan, sort of. "There is a woman, a friend of my father's when they were younger. She left the Community a long time ago, but kept in touch with my parents, and I know they live downstate. Her husband's from Outside, and he never had any patience with Ray, even before this. Said he was a megalomaniac, that he didn't care about the Community at all, just what it could do for him.

"I think they would take us in, take care of Maggie, at least. They don't have any children of their own, and Maggie was named for her. I'd… I have skills, I'd get a job. I hadn't really thought beyond that."

In the panic while gathering their things, while she'd made her hasty plans, it had seemed a good idea to go to Meg, someone who understood where she was coming from, and what she would need to do to live in the outside world. Then she had thought only that Meg and her husband could have helped them, taught them, given Maggie the background she would need to grow up away from the Community.

Now…her nerves were tingling, and the more she listened to them the worse it got. "There's something going on, something more than I thought at first. It's not just a power grab—that doesn't make sense. If Ray's willing to use force to take us back, willing to involve the outside authorities, the bad publicity that would bring, I'm not sure I can just run away and try to pretend it wasn't happening. I just can't bring anyone else into it. Not even you."

"What do you mean?" Josh scowled, running one hand through his hair in exasperation. "Elizabeth, I think you need to tell me what's going on. Let me decide what risks I'm willing to take, all right?"

She wanted to refuse him, to take Maggie and run. The last time she had told anyone what she feared… The memory of Cody's face, slack and uncomprehending above the rope around his neck, made her stomach heave, and she thought she was going to be ill all over the carpet. He hadn't been able to deal with it, had left her alone with this. Or…Ray had killed him, to keep him from helping Elizabeth, to isolate them even more. She hadn't wanted to believe it, caught between two horrible truths, but the possibility had to be faced.

What was Ray capable of? If she knew what he was planning, she might understand. But she had no clue.

"Elizabeth?"

Her silence had clearly sent the wrong message, because an expression of hurt passed over Josh's square-boned face. "You can trust me. Maggie wouldn't have called me if I wasn't to be trusted."

His logic didn't follow; Maggie called squirrels and raccoons and in one rather startling instance a half-grown black bear. None of them were to be trusted except to follow their own nature. What was the nature of a…a were-unicorn?

To be faithful, and true, a little voice told her. To protect and defend, fierce as any lion.

Joshua wasn't Cody. He was a grown man, used to taking care of himself. Nobody would slip a rope over his head and hang him from a tree; he would kill before he let himself be killed that way.

Elizabeth, you know he was ill, depressed after everything that happened. Ray, after the funeral, when she had blurted that she didn't believe he would kill himself. *It's a tragedy, of course, but your accusations… It's dangerous to make people doubt the truth that way.*

Yes. It would have been dangerous to suggest that Cody hadn't thrown the rope over that branch by himself. That it wasn't coincidence that, the day after she had shared her suspicions about Ray with her best, oldest friend, he had killed himself. Dangerous to even think that he had been killed so that she and Maggie would be left entirely on their own.

"Elizabeth?"

"My name is Libby." She looked at him, and in her exhaustion and worry it was as though the man was overlaid by the beast, a shimmering outline of white and gold, the only thing the same those deep brown eyes watching her, fringed by a lock of shaggy blond hair. The phantom horn dipped, and she could almost feel the sharp tip of it touch her face, light as a caress. "My family calls me Libby."

"I think you're always going to be Elizabeth to me," he said, and there was a meaning in his voice that she didn't quite understand. Nonetheless she felt herself blushing, and started talking again before she came to her senses.

"Maggie and I were raised in a separatist enclave called the Community. I know, it's clichéd, but when it was started, by our grandfather and some of his friends, they didn't think they needed a fancy name."

Her grandfather had been plain, in the Amish sense. No frivolity…but he had the most marvelous laugh, she remembered that. A laugh like warm water, and hands that could hammer a nail or hold a baby with equal care. Her father's laugh had been the same; her mother was quieter, but she had a way of looking at problems that made them almost solve themselves, without her ever getting fussed or worried. Like the way she brushed Elizabeth's hair, the knots almost sliding apart on their own, like…

Like magic.

The thought occurred to her, and she paused, then shook her head at her own foolishness. Her mother had been a thoughtful, pragmatic woman with a skill for seeing solutions, that was all.

"We're not isolationist—we go to the county schools, and we trade with the local farmers and stores, stuff like that. It's not a cult. People come and go as they like, but most people stay. My parents were born there. Maggie and I were born there."

Josh nodded, as though he understood. Maybe he did. He grew up in a herd, he'd said. He knew the bonds that family could put on you.

"We did have...quirks, though. The purpose of the Community was to stay away from the mass media as much as we can, not spend our lives online, simplify and pare down to what was really important—family and friends and living within our means.

"But it's changed." Her voice caught in her throat, and she had to stop a moment to collect herself. "Small ways at first. Things I didn't even see at the time, but looking back now I can see a pattern. More strangers in town, and people leaving without a word." Like she and Maggie had done, she realized. Had they, too, been driven out?

"Then last autumn, in October, a bad strain of flu hit us. Really bad. We don't have a hospital, just a little clinic, and by the time our doctors knew what was going on...a lot of people died. Including our parents—and Shawna."

She paused a minute to remember Shawna: tiny, with a temper like the smiting of God—and a booming voice that could fill the entire meeting hall.

"Shawna led the Elders, sort of a city council. They're not all old, it's just a courtesy title. Someone with a sense of humor, I guess. They're elected from the adult population, and the leader is chosen by the other Elders. Usually the one with the best horse sense— sorry, you know what I mean. The one who was most practical, who could calm everyone else down, or see every side of an argument and decide impartially what to do." She recited the names from memory, as familiar with them as her own family—most of them were, in fact, members of her family, one way or another. "My grandfather had been the first, and then there was Micah, who died early, and then Eliza, who I was named for, and then Shawna.

"Shawna was leader for years—all Maggie's life. Everyone listened to her, even if they didn't agree with her." It still seemed impossible that she died. No virus, no bug should have been able to stop Shawna.

"After the epidemic passed, and we had to elect a new leader…there were only two Elders left who had enough experience, enough backing. Even though Ray was younger, he won. He had been courting support for years, I guess. He had been part of the emergency medical committee, the one that brought in extra doctors and supplies, convinced the Board of Elders to upgrade our facilities. People were convinced he could do no wrong. That was when I—"

"Noooo!"

Elizabeth was already moving by the time Josh recovered from the sudden, pained yowl, but they both were at the bedside in seconds. He waited, while she took the shaken, still-sleeping girl in her arms, rocking her slowly to wakefulness.

"It's all right, Maggie, it's all right, baby, it's all right," Elizabeth crooned. "It's just a bad dream, only a dream, and we're here, we're here."

Hesitant, as though he were afraid of the reaction he might get, Josh reached his hand out and touched the top of Maggie's head, letting his pale fingers rest lightly on her dark hair.

Between the unicorn's touch and her sister's embrace, slowly Maggie stopped sobbing. With a faint, painful hiccup, she wiggled out of their reach and scooted up against the headboard. They let her, sensing a need for distance now, not comfort.

Her eyes were wide, staring past them into something only she could see, and her hands shook as she wrapped them around her knees.

"The bad animals. They're coming."

Chapter 7

Elizabeth felt panic clutch her throat at Maggie's words. *No. Not now.* Maggie wasn't a dreamer. She was just stressed, that was all, it was her imagination using what she knew—animals—to express her fear. That was all.

"Oh, baby…"

Maggie shook her head, refusing her sister's attempt to soothe her, or tell her it was only a nightmare. "They're real, Elizabeth. They are, I know they are. I can see them and I can hear them…and they can hear me, too." Her face was red-mottled with tears and frustration, and her voice hitched as she spoke. Elizabeth felt the ever-present fear crawl back into her throat.

"It's all right, Maggie." Josh sat on the edge of the

bed across from Elizabeth and put his hand out. After a moment of hesitation, Maggie took it.

"You know what I am."

She nodded, a little uncertain.

"You know what I am," he said again, and her nod was more emphatic this time.

"What am I?"

"You're…" She cast a look at her sister, as though checking to make sure that it was all right to say what she wanted to say. Elizabeth had an idea where Josh was going with this, and gave an encouraging nod.

"You're a unicorn. A were-unicorn."

Josh nodded, his pale hair picking up the glints of light from the lamp, and when he tilted his head, Elizabeth could see the ghost echo of the Mustang again, the golden mane and bone-white horn. "I'm a Mustang. I am strong and fierce and my hooves can crush a wolf's skull if he is foolish enough to threaten my herd. My horn can toss a catamount a dozen paces, if he so much as snarls at a foal. And I am smart enough to outwit the cowboys who tried to rope us and treat us like pack animals. No bad animal will harm you, while I have the breath to move."

Elizabeth felt something press inside her chest, and tears welled in her eyes. His words sounded overblown, but he spoke simply, calmly, without any dramatics, and the truth in those words was like a deep church bell chiming. She could see the stress in Maggie's slender body starting to fade.

She could trust him. They both could trust him with their lives.

"Libby?" her sister asked, not looking away from Josh's face.

"Yes, baby?" she asked.

"You have a plan?"

Elizabeth swallowed at the trust in her sister's voice, and, for the first time ever, lied to her.

"Yes, baby. I have a plan."

Reassured, Maggie let them settle her back, this time actually tucking her under the coverlet.

"But where will you sleep?" Maggie asked, her eyes already closing again.

"Mustangs sleep standing up," Josh told her. "Everyone knows that."

Maggie giggled at the thought, and snuggled down into the pillow, as secure as if she were back in her own bed, surrounded by familiar walls. Elizabeth adjusted the coverlet, and looked across the bed at Josh, suddenly aware how very…domestic the scene was.

He tilted his head to indicate that they should move away. Reluctant to leave Maggie but even more loath to risk waking her, Elizabeth followed. To her surprise he opened the door to the room and went outside. She followed, blinking a little at the sudden sunlight, and closed the door gently behind her. The motel rooms were ranged along the narrow, badly paved parking lot in a slight angle, she noted suddenly, so that you could see every door clearly, no matter where you stood. All the doors were closed, the curtains all drawn.

There was only one car in the lot, down at the other end of the row, and another car pulled up to the manager's office, a little wooden outbuilding where Josh had gotten the key. If anyone came toward them, from either side of the road, they would have enough time to go back inside before they were seen.

And nobody knew they were there. The manager had only seen Josh. Still, her shoulders ached from tension. *Bad animals.*

There was a bench in front of their room, and he sat on it, patting the plastic surface next to him to indicate that she should join him. Reluctantly, she did.

"Has she had this sort of dream before?" he asked.

"Once," Elizabeth admitted. "Just before illness swept the Community." She didn't want to relive those terrible days, but they came to the fore anyway. "Everyone was so sick, so…we did everything we could, and people died anyway. Maggie was sick, too, running this terribly high fever, and she had the same nightmare then—she was convinced that 'bad animals' were coming, wanting to eat her."

Her own dreams had been less clear, but no less fearsome—and unlike Maggie's fever dream, she knew that they were true. Foreboding and doubt, the branches of a bare tree dappled in sunlight, the smell of freshly dug graves and a stink of something that wasn't quite anything she had ever smelled before. They all came true, every single fear, every single image. Was there anything she could have done to stop it? Elizabeth didn't think so…but she didn't know for sure. And she didn't know which was worse: inevitability, or the chance to change things slipping from her because she didn't know what to do.

"Maggie's never been afraid of anything before, not ever, and especially not animals."

"And that's why you ran? Because of the changes you mentioned, and Maggie's fear?"

"No. I…" She looked at her hands, watching them twist together as though they belonged to someone else. Inevitable? Or could she, somehow, change what was going to happen? Could she do more than run? He was a stranger, someone who had resented being pulled to their aid…and yet the memory of the way he had spoken to Maggie made her continue.

"I told you, about Shawna dying, and Ray being voted up. About how after that…things changed. People, some people started looking at us—at Maggie and me and some of our friends—differently. Factions were forming, sides being chosen, but there wasn't anything *happening* that I could point to. I had a bad feeling…."

Even as she spoke, Elizabeth knew that she wasn't going to tell him about her own dreams, her forebodings. She felt bad about that—he had trusted them with the most amazing truth—but she had never even told Cody about the way her dreams came true, never mentioned it to her parents. Most days, she didn't even admit it to herself. Maggie knew. Maggie had always known.

"And all that made you pack up your sister and leave the only home you ever knew?"

She expected him to laugh at her, or call her foolish. It sounded foolish, said out loud. Something someone spineless would do: run, because a shadow crossed her path.

Instead, he leaned forward, his gaze intent on her face. "My people have immense respect for instincts, especially ones that warn us about danger. But you have to tell me. I can't protect you unless I know what it is that we're facing."

Listening to Elizabeth's story, Josh kept losing the thread, feeling the rut slamming against him, like a bird frantic to break out of his abdomen. Elizabeth wasn't a virgin, but she was female, very much an adult female, and it seemed that was enough to set it off. The itch to shift, to strike out at another male, to win a mate…ancient urges, all coming to the fore now, in one burning itch. The way her muscles flexed under that satiny skin, the shimmer of her hair, the low timbre of her voice as she spoke…

He couldn't let it distract him. He was in control here, not the rut, damn it. He took a deep breath, and forced it to stillness, but the pressure remained, making him hot and itchy and more shorter-tempered than usual. But underneath it there was an equal fire, cooler but no less determined: to protect this woman, and her sister. He clutched at that fire, preferring its cool burn to the hot, mindless itch of the rut.

"Tell me," he urged her, when she paused. Elizabeth was holding something back, and he needed to know what it was. Not that what she'd told him wasn't bad enough; the thought that she and Maggie had been left alone, in danger. Was there nobody else she could have turned to, nobody who would protect them, believe in them?

Sure, he'd been kicked out of the herd, but that was normal, and he'd always known that they waited for him, eventually, when his wandering time was done. That was traditional. This… Her story was wrong, and it outraged him, that cool heat burning higher, clearing his soul of the rut, if only for a moment.

A moment, and no longer. He shouldn't push her; he shouldn't be here at all, he should never have made that promise to Maggie. No matter how he held it off, the rut was still burning inside him, and if he couldn't take her, then it wanted him to leave this place and move on. If he didn't find a suitable mate—a virgin, someone who would be acceptable to the herd—he…

He didn't know what would happen. The only stallions who returned were the ones with brides, or who knew someone waited for them back home. The bachelors, the unmated males…nobody ever saw them, nobody spoke of them. Once you left the herd, there was only one way to return.

Nine years he had been a bachelor, roaming wherever the day took him, seeing every part of this country, meeting all sorts of people. But the freedom was over. He needed to find the proper mate. The rut told him that it was time, past time, and the urgency was rising every day he waited.

"Tell me," he said again.

"That's just it." She spoke so softly he had to lean even closer to hear. "I don't know. I don't know what's wrong, I don't know what we're facing, I don't even know that they're not right and I'm crazy, imagining things."

"Those men back there used violence to try to take you back. That alone says you weren't imagining things." He could feel the anger rising again, the urge to lash out with hoof and horn. It hadn't simply been Maggie's call that had made him act with such vigor, although her fear-driven summons had been part of it. The look on Elizabeth's face, the terror and determination to protect the younger girl, had hit him like a two-by-four. Her courage had driven him, as much as Maggie's distress. "Nobody would listen to you?"

"I told someone, a friend, about…about Ray, my worries about why he was hanging around Maggie. He died."

Her voice was bleak, the sadness in it tearing at Josh. "Died?"

"They said it was suicide. Maybe it was." Her voice said she wanted to believe that, wanted to believe a friend had abandoned her rather than believe that someone had killed him because of her words. Suddenly her hesitation to share her story made more sense.

"I'm very tough to kill," he told her, making it as much a promise as he dared.

She took a deep breath, seemed to come to another decision. "Ray always made me uneasy, the moment he came to the Community."

"He wasn't born there?"

"No." She shook her head, and the now-short strands swept along her chin, hiding her expression. "His mother came when he was…eleven, I think. She was the cousin of a member, Leigh, a friend of my parents. She was looking for a better place to raise her son. He's older than I am, so I didn't know him growing up. Everyone else likes him, his school friends all stand by him even now, but…I don't trust anyone nobody dislikes. It means that they're pleasing everyone. Honest people don't please everyone."

He smiled at that—he had never thought of it that way, but she was right. When you spoke your mind, you pissed off someone, somewhere. "And you think Ray…what? Was dishonest?" Was he embezzling the school funds, or…

"I think he looks at Maggie in a way that's not right. No, not that way," she rushed to assure him when his expression turned thunderous. "But… My parents trusted Leigh, and I think Leigh trusted Ray—and told him too much. About Maggie. I think that she told Ray what she can do. And he sees it not as a gift, but a tool."

Mustangs had been given that look for too many generations. He understood, completely. "And you? Why are they so determined to bring you back, as well?"

"I'm the handle that works the tool," she said bluntly. "Maggie will do anything for me. And I'll do anything for her." Their gazes met, and in hers he saw a resigned exhaustion that sealed his resolve: in the herd, they protected the young. The damned rut could damned well wait. There was no way he would leave the two of them alone, not until he knew that they were safe. There was no way he *could* leave them alone. He had given Maggie his word. He would see them to safety.

He reached out and touched her hand, meaning only to reassure her. Instead, that touch sent shivers through Elizabeth, shivers that he felt rebound through his body, as well. Hot and cold, intense electricity in his veins, on his skin. He waited, half-afraid, for it to awaken the rut. Instead, he felt a slow smooth warmth coating him, subduing the rut for the first time in weeks; the touch triggered another avalanche of images and sensations of her body writhing against his own, the warm, wet pleasures of her depths, and his cock hardened, but without the recent urgency or itch.

For the first time in weeks, he felt not irritable, but anticipatory, like a kid who knows that he's finally going to get the much-wished-for present for his birthday. It made no sense, but he savored it, anyway.

The moment drew out into an almost uncomfortable silence, broken when Elizabeth's mouth opened in a long, involuntary yawn.

"Oh. I'm sorry." Her cheeks flushed with dusky rose, and Josh grinned, relieved to have something to reduce the tension. So long as he could think of her as someone in need of protection, like her sister, the rut seemed to be appeased. That was the only explanation he could think of.

But he couldn't count on that holding for long. Especially if she hit the fertile point in her cycle. He knew that the way he knew where his elbow was; a natural extension of his being.

"You're just as tired as Maggie," he said softly, holding her gaze. "Why don't you go inside and get some sleep, too? We're not going anywhere for a few hours. By now anyone looking for you will have determined that you haven't gone to any of the local officials, and that you didn't buy a ticket at the bus station—" her gaze dropped, admitting that that would have been her next step "—and they'll hopefully assume that you're walking or riding your miracle pretty pony somewhere else."

She let the self-mocking reference go, still too worried to be amused or distracted. "They won't come looking for us here?"

"That's why I made you guys wait outside when I rented the room," he reminded her. "Cash means they can't trace me, and waving around my description, even if they have it, won't make a difference—I have no connection to you, and have a history of traveling alone, so they'd have no reason to twig. And if they do come looking…" He reached out and tilted her chin up again so that she had to look at him. Her dark eyes were wide and the pupils dilated slightly, and her soft lips were open slightly again, showing just a hint of her slightly uneven white teeth. The rut battled again with his herd-protector instincts. Herd won. He didn't kiss her.

But oh, he very much wanted to. Kiss her, and do far more.

"I meant what I said to Maggie. If anyone comes here, if anyone threatens you…I will be here." He only hoped that they didn't change tactics and bring guns. He was tough, but not even Mustang hide was impervious to bullets, silver or otherwise.

"Go on, get some sleep."

Elizabeth balked. "What about you? You didn't sleep at all last night, did you? And don't give me that crap about sleeping standing up. I grew up in the country, I know damn well that horses lie down to sleep, and I suspect unicorns do, too."

"Not when we're on guard, we don't," he said. "Now go, shoo."

"You're not going to stay out here all day," she said, standing up and reaching for his hand again, as though forgetting the shiver that had rocked them both just a minute before. "That's silly, and also dangerous if one of Jordan's men sees you in your other form—they're not about to forget the horse that nearly neutered them."

She paused. "Unless you'd be more comfortable that way? I...I don't..."

She spluttered to a stop and then glared at him, her lips pursed and her glare sharp, and her body language showed exasperation, one hand fisted on her hip, shoulders back and pointed chin jutting forward.

"This is all really weird to me, Josh, and stop laughing, because I can tell that you're laughing at me. Do were-unicorns prefer to sleep in four-legged form or two?"

He didn't want to. He really didn't want to. But there was no way to avoid it, not with the rut still itching hotly inside him and Elizabeth standing in front of him, indignant and brave and befuddled and elegantly adorable. He took her hand, and pulled her onto his lap, his other arm coming up to cup the back of her head and bring her closer so that he could taste that mouth properly.

Once their lips met, the rut exploded. Her skin was smooth and smelled like apples and pine and a slightly waxy taste of the hotel soap, and underneath it all the deeper unmistakable musk of a woman. He was hard immediately, painfully so, wanting only to tumble them both to the cracked pavement, in public, and claim her then and there.

He restrained himself, not letting the rut win, but his hold on her tightened and he plundered that sweetly tangy mouth with teeth and tongue, drawing incoherent but not unhappy murmurs from her throat. Her fingers closed over his shoulders, digging into the flesh, and he felt her entire body lean into him.

"Josh." His name was neither protest nor encouragement in her mouth, more as though she was tasting the word itself, finding him within those four letters. Josh, not Mustang.

The sound of a car coming down the road reached them both at the same time, and they released each other, moving apart quickly and turning like one creature to watch the car. Her body was poised for flight, his strained to shift—he could protect her better with hooves than he could with hands.

But the car kept going, not even slowing down as it passed the motel, and they both let out near-identical sighs of relief.

Elizabeth watched the car disappear around the turn in the road, not able to meet Josh's eyes. The way she had reacted, what must he think of her? It was as though think-it-through Libby had disappeared utterly, as though she had never existed.

"That was... I'm sorry," he said, his voice oddly rough.

"That was very nice, and I'm not." She got up from the bench again, but this time didn't offer him her hand. "The offer still stands. To share the room, I mean. Unless you'd be more comfortable outside?"

He probably would, she could see it in his face. But he shook his head. "I'd be more comfortable keeping you two in sight. If you could loan me one of those pillows…?"

They went inside, walking quietly so as not to wake Maggie. Elizabeth paused by the edge of the bed, watching her sister, who was snoring gently, a peaceful expression on her face now, as though dreaming of something sweet.

Her fingers lifted to her own mouth, still feeling the tingle of Josh's mouth on hers. It had been instinctive on his part, probably foolish on hers, but she savored the memory anyway. Everything had been worry and fear for so long, she had almost forgotten how to just have a moment of pure pleasure.

Elizabeth slipped a pillow out from under the coverlet and handed it to him before pulling off her sweatshirt and slipping under the covers with her sister, wearing only a T-shirt and sweatpants. She turned onto her side, her hand curled under her cheek, and watched him put the pillow down on the floor and try to adjust his length comfortably on the thin carpet. Immediately she could tell that wasn't going to end well. Sure enough, within minutes he gave up, got up and settled himself in the chair by the door instead. He propped the pillow against the wall behind him to provide a comfortable headrest, his legs splayed out on front of him.

She knew the feeling of those legs, that firm chest, the heat of his hands, as well as she knew the feel of riding on his back, her fingers curled into his mane, and the two seemed to blend in her emotions, making her stomach flutter and the apex between her legs heat up in anticipation. Her brain was torn in two directions: the intense physical contact they had just shared, the warm sense of anticipation curling low in her stomach, against the fear and concern about the men hunting them, and the worry of what their next move should be. Deciding that neither one was anything she could do anything about right now, she asked another question instead.

"You never did answer Maggie's question," she said quietly. "Are you a unicorn who changes into a man, or a man who changes form?"

He winced, as though she'd hit on a sore point, and she fully expected him to tell her to go to sleep and stop pestering him. But instead, he answered.

"There's enough non-Mustang blood in the herd now, we're born two-legged. Then after a few weeks, we make our first change. It's a big party, sort of like a first birthday." His voice was low, but she could hear the fondness in it, as he remembered simpler days. "We switch back and forth pretty evenly when we're kids, and then mostly stay two-legged as teenagers."

He stopped, and she wanted to get him to continue, fascinated by this impossible, fantastical world he was showing her.

"It's where we learn to be human—we are human, in all the ways that count. We have the same social cues, the same cultural history. Just…a little different. We go to school, date, get part-time jobs and make our parents crazy. After that, the females have a pretty normal life.

They go to college or learn a trade, get jobs, settle in.... The males get kicked out."

She made a noise of protest and he glanced up at her. "Oh, not like that. It's more…the herd is built around females. We're like horses in that regard, at least—a stallion might do the hard kicking, but the oldest, wisest woman, the one with the most experience, makes the decisions. So when we're young and prone to challenging everything that moves, we get sent out to do our damage elsewhere, and come back when we've had some sense nipped into us."

She could tell that there was more to it, but exhaustion was creeping up on her, abetted by the surprisingly comfortable mattress and the feel of her sister's sleeping body that had—the moment Elizabeth got into bed—curled instinctively against her back.

"Go to sleep," he said, gently. "I'll tell you more when you wake up."

And with that promise, and the memory of his mouth on hers, she drifted off into a peaceful sleep.

Despite the surprising comfort of the chair, Josh found it impossible to sleep himself, and once he was certain that Elizabeth was soundly in the grip of her dreams, he got up and made the shift. There was barely enough room for him to move, between bed and desk, but he found it easier to think in this form. There were fewer options, fewer distractions. Fight or flight? Choose one, and act on it.

Interestingly, the rut quieted when he was this self. It was still there, an instinct surging within him, but when all your moods were instinct based, not depending on rational thought, it was easier to deal with and control them. It was dangerous, too. He could feel that, even though nobody had ever told him so, specifically. The longer the rut went on, the more the drive to find his mate drove him, the stronger the urge to shift to four legs, where things were simpler, morality black-and-white: survival or death. The two-legged form was limiting, slow and weak. No mate would ever willingly choose that, and if he didn't find a mate…

That was the thing never spoken of, he realized suddenly. The thing boy-children were never told. The reason why so many young stallions never returned to the herd. His four-legged self understood what his two-legged self refused to acknowledge. If he didn't heed the rut, didn't find the Pure One, the lifetime mate, he would become a bachelor stallion; forever in four-legged form, never human again.

Mustang liked his four-legged form, but not always-and-forever.

The girl had called him. He accepted that now, in this self. It was a simple fact, not to be questioned. He had answered, and accepted them as herd, as responsibility. He watched them sleep now, remembering his dam sleeping the same way with one of his younger siblings. Family. The longing rose up in him, a loneliness that was wholly human matching the call of the rut, mixing into a bittersweet brew.

How could he choose between two such powerful pulls?

Elizabeth stirred, a little murmur escaping her as she slept, and he felt a surge, not in the rut, but that softer, gentler but still intense emotion. He shoved it down. The rut was cleaner, more understandable, more manageable. His two-legged form might be confused but he knew the truth: Mustangs chose women without family ties, without past experiences. Virgins. That was the way it had always been.

For the first time, watching Elizabeth sleep, he wondered *why*.

Chapter 8

The sky was pale blue above her. Elizabeth lay on her back, the smell of fresh grass and roses surrounding her, and stared at the blue as though it was the most magical thing she had ever seen. That sense of peace, of contentment, wrapped itself around her like the pair of arms that held her close, a warm chest at her back, the sound of someone whispering in her ear. She couldn't make out the words, didn't recognize the voice, but she was so calm, so comfortable, that she didn't feel any desire to turn and see who the speaker was. It was enough to be there, to float under the blue sky, and not have any worries....

Except she did. Even in the dream, Elizabeth could not let go of reality, and it reached for her, cracking the blue sky and reaching with putrid gray limbs, clawed fingers clutching at her. The wind turned cold, and the arms slid away, even as she was turning, trying to find them, trying to escape the claws looking to rend her apart....

The dream faded, blue skies and clawed beasts swirling into the rise to consciousness, and she woke to the faint pink light reaching through the window, under the curtains, feeling completely disoriented. Where was she? What time was it?

The sound of her sister's soft snores reassured her—wherever they were, they were together. Then the room came into focus, and she saw Josh sitting in the chair, watching her. His face was in shadows, but she could still make out the line of his chin, the strong nose that echoed the lines of his equine form, the stubble on his chin....

Well, that answered a question she hadn't thought to ask. Unicorns needed to shave. Now that she thought about it, there had been a faint shadow of beard at the end of his muzzle in his other form, too.

It took her a few tries to get the words out, her mouth was so dry, but she finally managed. "What time is it?"

"Almost five—" he paused "—a.m."

She sat up fast at that, the cover falling off her shoulders, and Maggie made an incoherent protest, waking up more slowly.

"Wha's wrong?" she asked her sister, her voice thick and groggy, not really alarmed.

"Nothing, Maggie," Josh said. "It's all right." To her,

he said, "I know it wasn't the plan. But you two needed the sleep. You were exhausted. And nobody came by at all, not even slowing down as they drove past. We're all right."

She didn't doubt that he had sat there, all afternoon and through the night, watching out for them. Still, the lost time made her pulse race: who knew what had happened while they slept?

"I moved your clothing into the bathroom," he said, still not moving, just watching her. "Go, shower. You have time."

No. She didn't. She really didn't. Elizabeth didn't know what was fueling her certainty, but she wasn't going to question it, not now. Not when it had kept them free and ahead of Ray's men, so far.

And yet, Josh was right. For now, they were safe. She had time to catch her breath, take a longer shower than she'd allowed herself the night before, time to figure out what they were going to do rather than merely keeping half a step ahead.

Shower, maybe some breakfast, and then she could think about the next step.

The hot water hitting her scalp calmed her nerves somewhat, and she could feel her body waking up, supporting what he had said: the difference in how she felt this morning, after a full night of sleep in a real bed, was significant. Hopefully Maggie would feel as alert and awake this morning, the nightmares of the night before forgotten.

Her own nightmare still lingered, and she tried to reconstruct it, as much from habit as anything else. The blue sky and sense of peace…the momentary safety they had found here? The gray arms, the clawed hands… She shuddered even under the hot water. Her brain was giving form to the uncertainty, that was all. No arms were going to reach down from the sky to grab her. Even with everything else that had happened, that was…silly.

She soaped up her body and rinsed, then she lathered shampoo into her hair. The shortness of it took her by surprise—there was so much less of it to wash, now, and the weight difference still threw her—then she lathered up again, just for the ability to do it. After the past few days she would never take hot water and shampoo for granted, not ever.

The events they'd gone through seemed distant, now, under the pounding curtain of hot water. Had she really fought, physically, with Jordan? Slept outside under the trees, without a tent? Kissed a man she barely knew—a man who wasn't even human?

Sliding the washcloth over her skin, she thought about Josh. The motion wasn't sexual, at least not at first. But the sense of peace that had filled her while she slept, and the memory of his gaze on her as she woke, warm and intent, slowly changed her thoughts from innocent to…less innocent. The roughness of the cloth became the calloused feel of his palm, the scratchy stubble of his cheek. It had been too long since she'd felt someone else's touch—a year, since before her parents fell ill and the care and protection of her sister became her burden alone.

His kiss had been fierce, hot, sudden. Would he have a gentle touch as a lover? Or would he be more force-ful, more aggressive? She could sense both sides in him, gentle and fierce. She had seen both aspects... would passion bring the stallion to the fore? Would he coax a response from her, slow and sweet, or demand it, up against the tiles, the water pouring down over them both....

Oh.

The sensation of his mouth on hers was as real as if it were happening again, then she felt those lips slide down her neck, nibbling at her shoulder, as she swept the cloth down, over her breasts until the nipples ached, they were so swollen. Would he suckle there, like that? Her head tilted back, and her body arched, as though offering herself to the not-quite-phantom lover, and—

"Libby?" The door opened, and a wave of cold air entered the bathroom ahead of her sister. "Libby, I gotta pee."

Elizabeth dropped the washcloth, flustered, and then sighed. "Just don't flush until I'm done," she warned her sister. Although, she admitted to herself, a blast of cold water might be exactly what she needed. How did just the thought of him wipe everything—every worry, every fear—out of her head? Her hormones hadn't controlled her brain since she was nineteen.

She rinsed the last of the shampoo from her hair, and turned the water off. Maggie, at the sink washing her hands, leaned over to flush the toilet, and then handed one of the towels to her around the shower curtain.

"Did you leave me any hot water?"

"No."

She got dressed quickly, putting on her old jeans that had been airing out overnight, and topping them with the new sweatshirt. The newly short strands startled her again, when she instinctively tried to finger comb it out, and ran out of strands far too early.

"This is going to take some getting used to," she muttered, then looked at herself in the mirror, having to wipe the steam away with an edge of her towel. Her eyes looked larger, her chin more prominent, and her skin had a flush that she was pretty sure was more than just the heat from the shower.

"Baby, you want breakfast?"

A gagging noise was her answer: Maggie had stopped eating breakfast a few months ago, and Elizabeth had worried about it until she noticed that her sister was still eating normally the rest of the day. Apparently it was just in the morning that she couldn't stomach the idea.

When she came out into the main room, Josh wasn't there. The door was closed, and his pack was still on the floor next to his chair, so after the first flutter of panic, she didn't let his absence stress her. "He probably had to pee and couldn't wait for us to be done," she said out loud.

Going to her own pack, she reached in and rummaged through it until her fingers closed on the soft leather of her address book. It was a thin notebook, barely the size of her palm: she didn't know many people outside of the Community, and she had never needed to write down the addresses or phone numbers of people she saw every day, could walk to their house if she needed to speak to them. The leather cover was worn—she had owned it since she was Maggie's age, a birthday present from Cody—and it opened to the page she wanted, almost as though by magic, but more likely because she had been opening it to that page for two weeks since the dreams had turned more urgent, checking and rechecking obsessively to make sure that it was still there.

Under the D heading: Dolan, Margaret. The woman Maggie was named for. An old family friend, someone who knew the Community but was no longer part of it. Someone who had known and loved their parents. There were three phone numbers printed there, added over the years, but no address.

"Do it," she told herself. "Now, before you chicken out, or someone finds us or…" She ran out of possibilities, but didn't make a move toward the phone. "Do it now, before Maggie gets out of the shower."

That was incentive enough to get her moving. If this… If Margaret didn't answer, if the phone numbers were wrong or if she refused to help them—Maggie didn't need to know.

The first number rang seven times, then eight, before Elizabeth gave up on it. The second went to a voicemail message saying that Meg Dolan was out of the office, please leave a message. Elizabeth hesitated, and then hung up the phone. No messages. She had to do this person-to-person.

She dialed the third number with fingers that trembled slightly on the buttons. The door opened, and she looked up, started, but it was only Josh. His hair was wet, so she assumed he had gone to find his own shower as well as a toilet. She held up a finger when he opened his mouth to say something, asking him to wait. She wasn't sure she could focus on a conversation with him without forgetting what she had planned to say if someone picked up the phone.

One ring. Two. Three. She was starting to panic, wondering what she was going to do, if she would have to leave a message, when the ringing stopped, and a man's voice answered.

"Hello?"

It was a deep voice, sleepy and confused, and Elizabeth felt a sudden pang of guilt—she had forgotten it was still so early in the morning.

"I'm sorry," she said into the phone. "I'm trying to reach Margaret Dolan?"

"Meg? Right. Who may I say is calling?"

"I… It's Libby. Libby Sweet. Sean and Deborah's daughter Elizabeth."

She waited while the man tried to place the name and connection, then she heard the rustling of cloth— sheets?—and his voice, lower now, away from the mouthpiece. "Meg? Honey, wake up. There's a girl on the phone for you, says her name is Libby? Libby Sweet?"

There was a clutter, and then a woman's voice in Elizabeth's ear, sleepy but excited-sounding. "Elizabeth? Little girl, is that you? Oh, but not so little anymore! How is everyone? Why are you calling at this hour? Libby, what's wrong, what happened?"

If she let them start, the tears would overwhelm her. Elizabeth choked them back, pressing her fist to her mouth in an effort to keep sound from escaping until she could get control back.

"It's…it's a long story. I'm sorry to call you so early, but…Meg, we need help. Maggie and me. We need your help."

"Libby…your parents? Deb…"

Elizabeth could hear the awareness in the other woman's voice even as she asked the question.

"They're gone. I'm sorry, I… Last year…we had a flu virus, a bad one. They died within a week of each other."

"Oh, God. God rest their souls. And you need my help. Absolutely. What can I do?"

"We need a place to stay. Just for a little while."

"You've left the Community?" Meg sounded surprised but not terribly so, as though she'd expected something of the sort, eventually.

"We…needed some time away." That was all she was willing to say right now, all she was willing to admit to herself right now. The idea of never going home, even a home that had suddenly turned dangerous and unfamiliar, was too much for her to handle right then.

A warm hand came down on her shoulder, and Elizabeth shivered, the touch almost too much for her right now, triggering warm memories of her shower fantasy.

He seemed to realize that, somehow, because the hand lifted, and he retreated to the other side of the room. Meg was giving her directions on how to get to her home; Elizabeth had remembered correctly and it was only a few miles from where they were. Dimly, while she was reaching for the pad of paper and cheap motel pen on the nightstand, she heard Maggie come out of the bathroom, and Josh say something to her sister in a low voice. Maggie came to sit on the floor at Elizabeth's feet, her hair—still long and damp—hanging down her back. She had a comb in her hand that she used to clear out any remaining snarls, then started braiding it while Elizabeth got the rest of the directions.

"Yes. Yes, we'll be there soon. Lunchtime, for certain. Yes. Thank you. I can't wait to see you, too."

Elizabeth hung up the phone and, unable to look at her sister right then, instead raised her gaze to where

Josh leaned against the door. He was wearing a faded pair of blue jeans this morning, she noticed now, and a navy blue shirt that set off his tanned complexion and drew her gaze to the muscles cording his forearms.

It made sense, she supposed; he was probably solid muscle in this form as well as the other. The thought made her skin warm, so she looked up, away from his body, as though that would keep her from thinking about it. His hair was dried already, the color of corn silk, and once again she could sense the echoes of his unicorn-self over his features.

He looked worried, and she smiled to reassure him. "It's okay. Meg and her husband are thrilled, and have offered us a place to stay for as long as we need."

"Do I know them?" Maggie asked.

"No, baby, she left when you were too young to remember. But you were named for her. This is Aunt Meg."

"Oh!"

Maggie's entire knowledge of the woman was a card on her birthday, and the occasional present, but that was enough.

"She doesn't know what's going on?" Josh asked quietly.

"No." Elizabeth shook her head. "No. I… There was no way to tell her, over the phone, and…and maybe she won't need to know. Maybe Ray's given up."

She could tell from Josh's expression that he didn't think it was going to be that simple. Neither did she.

* * *

The neighborhood Meg directed them to was a quiet little cul-de-sac in a pretty neighborhood the next town over. Maggie had wanted Josh to change forms and have them ride there, but both Elizabeth and Josh pointed out that riding a unicorn through a suburban neighborhood wasn't quite the same as traveling through a state-owned forest, and might attract just a few stares. Maggie sulked for a little while, but finally agreed. By the time they got there on foot, though, Elizabeth wished they'd been able to ride—or could have rented a car. Or even bicycles. They had taken it as slowly as possible, but even wearing sneakers her soles and toes were aching, and she suspected Maggie was feeling it even worse, from the quiet, pinched expression on her sister's face. The younger girl had stopped making comments or trying to crack jokes almost ten minutes before, and her shoulders were drooping, despite the long rest.

Even Josh seemed to be feeling it. His stride was still long and easy, but he was quiet, too, and Elizabeth thought that he took every step more and more reluctantly. But why? Once they were safe with Meg and her husband, he would be free to leave. She got the distinct feeling that he couldn't wait to shake their dust off his heels…or hooves.

She wondered, suddenly, where he had been going when they met him, why he had been camping in that wooded bower, what journey he was on, where he came from…all the sort of things you'd learn about someone you met while traveling—assuming you weren't so focused on not being caught, or your sister's health, or…

Libby stopped to realize that she hadn't worried about her sister's health since… Since they met Josh. Unicorns…could they heal, too? She had a vague memory of something about their horns, but she had never been into fantasy as a child, and couldn't remember anything more. She thought about asking Josh, but the Mustang's face was so grim and distant, she couldn't find the words.

"That's it," she said instead.

"It" was the end house on the cul-de-sac; a two-story building made up of a center hall and two one-story wings on either side, neatly tended landscaping on either slide of a curved slate path that led from the driveway to the front door.

"And this is where I leave you," Josh said.

Even though it was expected, the words sent a pang of regret through Elizabeth. "I don't even know how to begin to thank you—" she started to say, and he cut her off brusquely.

"Then don't."

Elizabeth was taken aback by the return of his rudeness, but was distracted by the front door opening, and the appearance of a woman on the front porch. She was tall, with short gray hair sleekly styled around her head, wearing jeans and a bright pink sweater.

"Libby?" the woman asked, her tone incredulous. "Oh, God, Libby—and is that little Maggie?"

"Aunt Meg?" Maggie asked her sister in a cautious tone.

"Aunt Meg," Elizabeth confirmed, her legs carrying her across the lawn and into Meg's strong hug, completely forgetting, for a moment, the presence of their companion.

By the time she extricated herself, Maggie getting the same bear-hug treatment from the older woman, and turned back to look—he was gone.

Watching Elizabeth race across the lawn and into the woman's embrace, her sister following, Josh felt an odd twinge, almost of regret. They had filled his life so completely, it was hard to believe that three days ago he had not known of their existence.

The twinge was quickly swamped by the reemergence of the rut, as though it had merely been waiting for him to divest himself of his herd obligation before forcing him forward again.

Find a mate, the hot itching thing in his rib cage told him. *Find a mate or be forever trapped...forever alone.*

Mustang touched two fingers to his forelock in salute to the girls and their new home, and walked away. By the time he had reached the end of the street, the urge to shift overwhelmed him, even in the middle of this suburban tract, and he dropped his pack and let his muscles surge, melting and reforming with the burning ache that always accompanied the shift.

The four-legged form felt right, felt more solid and comfortable than his two-legged self, and part of him worried about that. He had told Elizabeth the truth: he was a man, not a horse, and while both sides were his true self, he had always been man first. Now…he wasn't so sure.

The sound of his hooves on the pavement made him uneasy, and he stepped delicately onto the grassy lawn, comforted by the softer, springier surface. He needed to get back to the forest, to somewhere less populated…. But how was he to find a mate there? Contrary to his recent experience, one didn't find young women wandering in the woods.

A muffled noise made his ears twitch backward and his tail flick once. Before his brain could process the sound, he was pivoting on his back hooves, leaving divots in the unlucky lawn, and racing—not away from the dangerous noise, but toward it. Back toward the house where he had just left Elizabeth and Maggie.

Chapter 9

One thing the myths and legends tended to warn about was the sheer power behind a charging unicorn. That was one thing they got right; especially a unicorn in the throes of the rut. The nice white door of the nice suburban house shattered under the second blow of the Mustang's hooves, and he was through the splintered remains without hesitating, following the scent of Elizabeth's anger and Maggie's terror.

He took the scene in with a hot-eyed glare and then, head lowered, slammed his horn into the man holding Elizabeth captive, skewering him through the shoulder and tossing him aside like a sack of grain. The human landed with a thump on the carpeted floor, and tried to crawl away, then stopped with a groan of pain, rolling onto his side and clutching at his shoulder. He tried to sit up, and the Mustang pulled back, lifting one hoof in clear threat. The man fell back to the floor, and didn't move again.

The woman who had taken the girls in stood to one side, and he could smell her confusion turning to fear. Had she allowed this? He stepped toward her, head still lowered, the tip of his horn bloody and gruesome, and she screamed, fluttering her hands as though to ward him away.

There was a noise behind him, and he turned to face the other dangers in the room, still keeping a strand of awareness on the wounded threat. There were two other men in the room, not men he had ever seen before, and one of them held a gun, the matte black mouth pointed directly at the Mustang. Infuriated, still riding a battle high, the Mustang went for that human first, generations of genetic memory of dealing with horn-hunters and cowboys driving his hooves as he struck.

Shock was still on his side, but the man got a shot off before the blow landed; the bullet whizzed past his ear and embedded itself in the ceiling. Fury took over; his hooves came down on the man's gun hand, shattering delicate bones, and another blow knocked the man to the ground, where the Mustang trampled him without hesitation. That human had pointed a gun at him; that human had threatened his herd. Rattlesnake, cougar or human; there was no answer to that save death.

There was a small part of his brain, still human, that regretted the violence, but it was easily silenced.

One human left—where had it run to? Mustang reared back, barely missing the chandelier hanging from the ceiling, now decorated with plaster dust from the bullet, and pivoted again on his hind legs, searching for the remaining threat.

"It's all right," Elizabeth called to him, her voice quavering, but strong. "I've got it."

The sound of her voice penetrated his fury faster than the sight of her on top of the third man, him face-down and her knee across his neck, clearly putting all her weight on it. He was already starting to move his arms against the floor, trying to find leverage to throw her off.

"Maggie, hurry!" she called. "Find rope!"

Maggie's voice floated back from another room, slightly desperate. "I'm *looking!*"

"Oh, my God, you killed Stephen!" The woman named Meg was hyperventilating. "You killed Stephen. In my house."

The woman had an excellent grasp of the obvious, Mustang noted, even as Maggie came back, triumphant, with a roll of duct tape in her hands.

"Meg, shut up and either help or sit down and stay out of my way," Elizabeth snapped, clearly furious. "And you, stay down!" She dug her elbow into the small of his back, making him go flat again with a pained *oomph.*

His Elizabeth had very sharp elbows, Mustang noted with approval. "You bastard. Did Ray send you? Did he?"

"He doesn't like being told no," the man said, grunting a little around the words. "Better us than what he'll send next."

"Screw you."

Maggie tore off a foot-long strip of tape and got it around the man's hands, binding them tightly—at what looked like a painful angle—behind his back. Elizabeth let up her pressure slightly, only long enough for the girls to flip him on his side and attach another strip of tape over the man's mouth, careful not to cover his nose. Then Elizabeth got the tape and walked over to where the injured man was still cowering, obviously convinced that the slightest movement would attract the beast's attention again. He was right. Mustang lowered his horn, ready to finish the job.

"No," Elizabeth said, sharply. Her back was to him, and Mustang wasn't sure if she was speaking to the attacker or him. But he took a pace back, giving her room to work without moving too far away. If the man made a single move that Mustang didn't like…

Elizabeth bound a strip of tape around his ankles, immobilizing him, then taped his hands together, in front of his body to limit the stress on the wounded shoulder.

The obvious attackers were down or neutralized. But what about the woman? Was she friend or foe? Did she call these men here? He took a step forward, intending to shift, in order to question her.

Elizabeth looked up and met his gaze, shaking her head slightly. *Stay in form.*

Apparently a horse with a horn was more intimidating than a shape-changing man. Since he felt more confident of his fighting ability with hooves than hands, he flicked his ears at her in agreement.

"You killed him," Meg said again, her eyes wide, as though she didn't quite understand the words she was saying.

"They were trying to kidnap Maggie," Elizabeth said, bitterly. "And you were going to let them. You lured us here, told us it was safe, and then you let them in."

"I didn't… I didn't lure you. They have Douglas. They said… They promised…" The woman subsided under Elizabeth's scornful glare.

"Someone came in and took your husband, and you trusted their promises over your obligation to my parents? To their memory? You were going to let them take a little girl—" and for once, Maggie didn't object to being called little "—to save your own skin?"

The woman's eyes were wide, and her face was set in creases, but she didn't deny Elizabeth's accusation.

"We're leaving now," Elizabeth told her in disgust. "Wait an hour, then call someone at the Community to come pick them up. Let them deal with the body—and maybe they'll help you find where Ray stashed your husband."

Mustang wanted to object—you didn't leave rattlesnakes alive to attack again—but this wasn't his call. And his Elizabeth, while fierce, wasn't a killer.

"You can't trust her," Maggie said, recovering from her scare, still sitting on the floor with the roll of tape in her lap. Her face was too pale, but her expression was just as fierce as her older sister's. "Put her in the closet. We'll call someone to let her out, once we're away." Maggie glared at the woman, outraged the way only an almost-teenager can be. "Maybe."

"Maggie. No."

Even as she scolded her sister, Elizabeth felt the idea's appeal. She had trusted Meg, had counted on her. Being betrayed like that was almost worse than the scare. If Josh—Mustang—hadn't charged in right then, they would be on their way back to the Community, even now.

"Why not?"

Her sister's pout was almost irresistible. Elizabeth resisted. "Because we don't know anyone to call to come and let her out, without giving away where we are. Unless we call the police, and that's not going to help us if we have to go to them later, no matter how we explain it."

"Oh." Her bloodthirsty side thwarted, Maggie played with the roll of duct tape and tried to think her way through to a satisfying solution.

"Better to just leave her here," Elizabeth said, aware of Mustang behind her, the solid bulk of his presence giving her strength to do what had to be done.

"In the closet?" Maggie asked hopefully.

"Not in the closet," Elizabeth said. "There's not enough room there, anyway. We leave them all here. Ray's men will check in at some point to see what happened to their people, or someone will see the door and call the police, if they haven't already." There had been no outcries or sirens, though; this was a residential neighborhood, and most people were either already at work, or in school. But they couldn't count on that calm lasting.

The hall closet actually did have room in it, testimony to someone's organizational skills. Maggie won: they shoved the surviving would-be kidnappers inside, leaving the door ajar just enough to let fresh air in.

They tied Meg to a straight-back dining-room chair with more of the duct tape, and shoved a washcloth from the bathroom in her mouth to keep her from calling out before they left.

"If the cops come by first, you'd better come up with a really good story," Elizabeth told her former family friend. "They're never going to believe a unicorn killed that guy."

"We should rob her, just to make it look right," Maggie said, a bloodthirsty spark in her voice.

"Maggie…" Elizabeth was starting to get annoyed with her sister, and her voice showed it.

"All right. But I'm getting food. It's lunchtime, and I'm starving. The least she can do is feed us."

While Maggie quickly went through the kitchen and gathered fresh fruit and sandwich fixings, and the Mustang kept a watchful guard over the bound would-be kidnappers, Elizabeth knelt down beside her former family friend and stared her in the eyes.

"I hope that they bring your husband back safely," she said sincerely. "I know my parents liked him, and you, and I don't want anyone else to get hurt. But I will never, ever forgive you for betraying us. Do you understand that? You will never be forgiven, you will never be able to tell yourself it's okay, that I understood, because I don't, and I won't. Ever."

A tear formed in the older woman's eye, and she nodded once, indicating that she understood. Elizabeth stood up. "Maggie! Let's go."

The Mustang stepped carefully through the wide doorway between living room and dining room to stand at Elizabeth's shoulder. The woman's eyes went even wider as the horn—now washed clean—lowered to rest directly against her chest. Something intense seemed to pass between them, and the tears fell unchecked.

Satisfied, the Mustang moved back and rested his chin briefly on Elizabeth's shoulder, the rough bristles there scratching even through the sweatshirt, and then stepped toward the now-shattered front door, out of sight of the bound woman. Maggie, still shoving food into her knapsack, followed without a backward glance.

Elizabeth paused a second longer, looking around at the house she had hoped would be a refuge. She had no idea what to do now, no idea where to go next. The only thing certain was that Ray was willing to resort to kidnapping—and violence—to get Maggie back…and she had to be willing to do the same to keep her safe.

By the time she walked outside, Josh had resumed his human form, and was checking a protesting Maggie for injuries.

"I'm fine! Stop worrying. You're as bad as Libby!"

"I just…"

His hands were shaking, and, as Elizabeth watched, her sister reached up to cover his hands with her own much smaller, more steady ones. "I'm fine. Libby's fine. But we have to get out of here, now. The bad animals are coming."

Neither of them asked what she meant, this time. They walked away, going as slowly and steadily as possible, only detouring to pick up Josh's pack. Maggie's usual exuberance was noticeably muted, hanging back to be close to the adults rather than, as was her usual wont, wandering away to look at whatever caught her fancy. Once they were out of the cul-de-sac, though, her normal demeanor seemed to return, and she went ahead a few paces to try to coax a large black squirrel down from the tree to sit on her shoulder.

They hadn't spoken to each other since leaving the house, and Elizabeth was afraid that Josh was angry at her for dragging him back in to rescue them once again, for the fact that she had misjudged Meg so badly, for… for everything and anything her mind could touch on. For not having a plan that would get them out of this mess, once and for all.

"I'm sorry," she said finally.

He stopped and stared at her. "Sorry? For what?"

"For… You shouldn't have had to come save us. Again. Maggie shouldn't have…"

"Maggie didn't. I knew something was wrong, I heard her scream." There was no way he could have, not through the walls of the house, the now-shattered door, not even in his Mustang form, and yet he had.

Elizabeth didn't seem convinced of that, more willing to believe that her sister had somehow forced him to do her bidding, and that drove him to ask her about it.

"I know that you don't like to talk about it, but what's the extent of her ability? Squirrels, bears…unicorns. What else can she call? And—" and there was the question he had to ask "—is it simply a matter of calling, or does she control the things she calls, too?"

Elizabeth could feel the quick succession of emotions flickering over her face, and she kept her eyes looking straight ahead so that he couldn't read anything in them. "She can't control animals. They're too…ephemeral. Their thoughts flicker and their emotions are too swift…she can call them, and ask them to do things, but there's no way to hold that for very long. She doesn't control them, just coaxes them."

Josh stopped and placed a hand on her arm. The touch was electric, but the look on his face was sobering. He had seen, anyway, or suspected. "That implies that there is something she can control. People?"

His voice wasn't angry or confrontational, but Elizabeth cringed anyway. Years of keeping it a secret, a thing never even thought, never whispered out loud, made the words stick in her chest. She didn't want to say anything more, too well trained to protecting Maggie. And yet, he had stood by them, had rescued them twice now, had his own incredible secret that he trusted them to keep—although, who would believe them if they tried to tell?—and she owed him the truth.

"Strong emotions are what she can catch at. If a person has very strong emotions, she can call them, too. And we hold on to our emotions longer than animals do." She had learned, from practically the moment Maggie was born, to keep her own emotions carefully controlled and even. "She would never do anything bad, or make someone do something against their will—" their parents had taught her ethics at a very young age, to prevent just that "—but when she was younger, we used to have to be careful, all the time.

"Now…I think she's a little scared of it. Which isn't a bad thing."

From the dawning look of understanding Josh's face, a great deal of Maggie's behavior—and Elizabeth's as well—suddenly made sense to him. "It could be useful, in self-defense. Back there in the house, if she could have controlled the men—"

He wasn't saying anything she hadn't already thought of. "She's thirteen. I don't want her carrying that kind of weight on her shoulders. There's enough…"

Her voice trailed off as everything that *she* had been carrying around rushed back, the events of the past few days fading under the memories, and she almost doubled over under the weight.

"Elizabeth? Libby?" His shoulder brushed hers as he moved closer, and she breathed in the scent of his skin, that same musky, slightly musty scent that his other form carried, but underlaid now with a more seductive hint of human male. She straightened, intending to insist that everything was fine, but then his hand sought hers, warm fingers twisting with her colder ones, and she couldn't form the words. He knew it wasn't fine, knew what Maggie was, what she could do, what they were facing. He knew almost everything.

Almost.

As they walked along the quiet street, the sound of traffic on the main road getting closer and closer, she made her final decision.

Elizabeth started to talk, softly, barely even aware that she was doing so. "When I was growing up, things were different. The Community was such an open place…we were all misfits, one way or another, choosing to be out of step with the outside world. I went to public school, but I loved coming home every day, spending my weekends not watching TV or being online but getting outside, getting my hands dirty, or reading. When Maggie was born, even when we realized what she could do, we didn't exactly broadcast it, but there wasn't any real concern, either. Maggie was special, but she was safe. Being good with animals wasn't so unusual." She smiled, a little sadly. "There were people, when I was growing up, who were just as odd, by most standards. Doctor Colleen, she always knew when someone was hurt, even before they got to the clinic. Sweetwater Jack could tell you how well your garden would grow, just by looking at how you'd planted. Things like that."

"It sounds like the Community was a special place."

Elizabeth nodded. "It was. Emphasis on *was*. I told you things were changing, going wrong. The past few years, even before the illness, the Community's been changing. People…aren't as open as they used to be, like there were secrets to be kept. Things to be scared of. Things…or people. Like it wasn't always safe to speak your mind. That's the world Maggie's been growing up in."

"And the 'bad animals' she said were coming? Who are they?"

"I don't know. I thought that it was just her picking up what was wrong, and saying it the only way she understood, but…" She took a deep breath. There were things she had never told her parents, never even told Cody. Had never told anyone, barely able to believe them herself, wondering if anyone else had seen them as well, if they, too, felt the unease and fear that was settling over the Community.

She had told Cody just her most surface fears, and he had either committed suicide rather than face them, or been killed for knowing too much. If she told anyone else…

But Joshua wasn't anyone else. He was a Mustang.

"I think I know what she's talking about. I'd hoped it wasn't true, hoped we'd both just imagined it, but it's either real or we're both going crazy."

"You're not crazy." His voice was soothing, calm, and for a moment she had a flash of blue sky, and the feel of a cool fresh breeze on her skin. "Tell me."

"It happened a little over a year ago, just before the flu struck. I ran a bakery, in the town center. Right across the street from the meeting hall. I'd go in early in the morning, before anyone else was awake, in order to be ready for the first rush of people wanting bread and bagels. And I felt…there were things following me, lurking. Things in the shadows. Even in the middle of the day I could feel something wrong, like spiders across my back."

"Survival instinct," Josh said. "Something was there, but you couldn't see it, so your mind was trying to warn you some other way."

She nodded. "Maybe. It went on for a few weeks, not regular, but enough to make me twitchy, uncomfortable. And most of those days I would come home and there would be Ray sitting on our porch. Just sitting. He wasn't a friend of my parents, but he was an Elder, and so I was polite—I'd submitted plans to enlarge the bakery, and one strong voice against it could kill the proposal. If he wanted to see what I would offer, to gain his support, it would make sense. But even then he made my skin creep. He would talk casually, to all of us, but there was noise under his words." She knew that didn't make any sense, but it was true.

"Noise?"

"Like he was saying one thing and a different thing, all at once. And I was the only one who could hear what he was saying, the second thing. He would make allusions to Maggie's skill, about the history of the Community, and I heard…something else. Not about the bakery, or trading support. Something darker.

"My parents didn't hear it." She didn't want to speak ill of her parents, didn't want to believe they were oblivious to the threat, but they had sat there and listened to him, and smiled and nodded without any sign of hearing what she heard. "They were wonderful people, loving and kind, but they assumed everyone said what they meant and meant what they said."

The snort Josh made at that could have come from the Mustang's muzzle.

"You have to understand, the Community was founded not just to get away from the outside world, but to make ourselves better. Mostly by increasing trust and kindness, but I think, back then, they had some idea of directing bloodlines by arranging marriages. That kinda fell apart pretty fast. You can't expect to raise independent thinkers and then have them accept that sort of thing." She managed to laugh. "My folks were hooked up by their parents, though. They used to tell me stories about their first date, how they were convinced they'd hate each other until they actually met."

She felt more than saw him smile, and the hand holding her own squeezed lightly.

"But Ray…he talked like he wanted to bring back those ideas, 'for the better result of the Community,' he said. And he'd…he'd hold Maggie up as an example of what could be achieved. He never said anything to suggest he knew but…he knew. And just listening to him made me feel like I'd waded through a pool of muck."

"Sounds like a bad animal to me," he agreed, and the steel in his voice didn't surprise her at all.

"You think he wants to use me," Maggie said, startling Elizabeth, who had thought she was far enough ahead not to have heard. "To do something bad."

"I…"

"It seems likely," Josh said calmly. "I don't know the guy, but his choice of hirelings doesn't leave me with the impression of a guy who only wants puppies and kittens and rainbows for everyone."

"He eats puppies for breakfast and kittens for lunch," Maggie said darkly. "And I'd kill myself before I let him get his hands on me."

"Maggie, don't ever say that!"

Her sister went pale, doubtless remembering, as Elizabeth was, Cody's funeral. Maggie reached back to hug her sister around the waist, burrowing her head against her chest. "I'm sorry" came out, muffled. "I didn't mean to…"

"I know, baby. I know. But don't say that, ever. Dying is not an option, you understand?" Elizabeth looked down at her sister, waiting until she saw her head nod in agreement.

Josh looked around, making sure that nobody was paying them any attention or watching from inside the houses still in view, then looked at the sisters, stock-still on the sidewalk. His nerves were calm for the moment, the rut had been sated, briefly, probably by his violent reaction to the kidnappers. But it was only a matter of time. The shift had happened so smoothly, almost too easily, and that was not good. His instincts were taking over, pushing him to find a mate, to finish the roving part of his life and rejoin the herd as a full—mated—member.

He wanted that, as much as he could ever remember wanting anything. He had left the herd full of excitement and wanderlust, but it called to him now, the rolling views and sweet grass of home, the sound of the yearlings at play, the way the lead mare would sit back and watch the world go by, nothing escaping her careful, wise eye.

His home was not like Elizabeth and Maggie's Community; they gathered only twice a year, and the rest of the time they scattered to their homes and jobs, their normal lives. But the time of the Spring Gathering was almost here, and he hadn't seen his people in nine years. If he didn't go now…

He would never walk among them again.

And none of that mattered. What Elizabeth had revealed to him, and his own experiences with the men sent after them, told him one thing: he needed to get them somewhere safe. Not just for now, but for always. And if doing that doomed him to a life on four legs… maybe that was what it meant to be a Mustang. If Elizabeth and Maggie were safe, he could accept that.

"What will you do now?" His brain was churning over the beginnings of a plan—a crazy plan, but a plan. But they needed to agree to it, first.

Elizabeth looked defeated, for the first time since he had met her. "I need to get Maggie somewhere safe. Then…I don't know. My parents were cautious and invested money outside the Community. I don't think Ray could know about it. It's enough for us to get by on, for a while. It will take a little time to get access to it, but I know how. Then I can worry about Ray. I just have to know Maggie's safe, first."

"I'm not leaving you!" Maggie objected, pulling away and staring at her sister as though she'd just been slapped. Her lower lip quivered, and her chin jutted up at a stubborn angle. If she'd been a yearling, Josh thought, she would have pricked her ears back, and swished her tail in defiance.

"Come home with me. The herd will protect you." The words slipped out before he could think about them, before he could frame them properly, or think it through.

"What?" Elizabeth looked shocked, and Maggie forgot to be angry, her pout turning to an open-jawed gape.

He didn't know if the herd would protect them, actually. Especially if they were seen as the reason why he was trapped in Mustang form. But Maggie would be safe with the bachelor herd, at least until she hit puberty. No member of the herd would hurt a child, but they would take any attempt to harm her as a personal insult—and a chance to prove themselves. And maybe, growing up in the herd, she would choose to be someone's virgin mate. Or not. But she would have a *choice,* freely made.

And Elizabeth… He swallowed hard at the thought of seeing her every day, of watching her through Mustang's eyes, of being with her but never being able to touch her….

But the thought of looking for another mate repulsed him. He didn't want a virgin stranger. He wanted Elizabeth.

And he couldn't have her. Not the way that mattered; not forever.

His decision took solid form, even as Maggie was nodding enthusiastically at her sister, begging her with eyes and voice to accept Josh's offer. It was best this way. Elizabeth would be safe, Maggie would be safe. That was all that mattered.

Chapter 10

The small office off the Community Hall was just large enough for a small desk and wheeled chair, four stacked file cabinets, and a table that held a coffeemaker and a pile of mugs. The two men standing before the desk had their backs to the wall—literally.

There was a long silence after they finished reporting that drew out past the socially comfortable and into the ominous. The two men did not dare shift or cough, although the one man's arm sling was clearly paining him, and the other had a nasty bruise on the side of his face, and what looked like a burn across his mouth, as though the skin had been roughly abraded.

Ray wasn't impressed by either injury. "You were overpowered—Stephen was killed—by two girls? Admittedly two smart and desperate girls, but really…"

The bandaged man started to speak, and glared at his companion when he tried to stop him. "I'm not going to be quiet, no. It happened and just because you got knocked out don't mean it didn't."

"What happened?" Ray's eyes narrowed, and he stared at the two men intently. "What did you leave out of your initial report?"

"Stephen didn't get killed by the girls...and the girls didn't do this to me." He indicted his bandage. "It was a beast. A monster."

"A monster." Ray was repeating the word, not asking a question, but the two men both became defensive.

"Not a monster. They had a horse with them," the first man said. "Same as the one they rode away on, near the woods. We told you about that."

"It wasn't a horse." The bandaged man was definite on that fact.

"A big goat then." His companion, equally stubborn, wasn't going to admit that anything out of the ordinary had happened, even if it meant that a girl and a woman had taken him down.

"It was a beast. A monster. It looked like a horse but it wasn't. It had horns, and its eyes were red, and they were smart. A horse has dumb eyes. This one looked right at me and there was an evil mind behind it, I swear." The bandaged man clearly didn't expect anyone to believe him, but he wasn't going to back down.

"And then it did that to you?" Ray asked, his voice neither scoffing nor convinced.

"It ran me through with that horn, threw me across the room. After it broke down the door and trampled Stephen. Did you look at his body? You think anything human did that? And it wasn't a horse, damn it. It was a..." He paused, unable to form the words his brain wanted to say, and then fell back on his earlier words. "It was a beast."

"It broke down the door coming in, not going out? Interesting." Ray looked away from the two men, staring instead at the wall behind them. "So it was outside, and came in to save them. She's getting stronger. No more birds and squirrels, not even someone's old plow horse, as I'd thought. A beast, you say? How very, very...useful."

He refocused on the two men in front of him. "We've tried doing this as quietly as possible, to spare the tender feelings of others here, but clearly that is no longer an option. We are ready to proceed to the next level of experiments. Maggie needs to be here, and she needs to be here now. I am tired of waiting.

"Michael, you're on injured reserve for now—get that wound rebandaged properly, and tell them I've authorized whatever painkillers you need. Dump the man, we don't need him any longer. Then start telling people that...hmm, that the girls were clearly under the sway of some outside force, some person or persons who had them captive, afraid and confused, and were willing to use violence to keep them, probably for some terrible reason you don't even want to imagine. That should spread easily, and people will add their own lovely touches, I am sure. Clive, I want you back on the trail. Take Meredith, and bring Set and the Dos with you."

"Sir?" Clive's tone was polite, but clearly dubious. "Are you sure? Take them outside the Community?"

Ray did not like being questioned, but he kept his voice calm, reassuring. "Meredith will keep them in check," he said. "And really, who better than those three to find our little beast-mistress?"

To that, Clive could only nod in agreement, and go off to find his new teammates.

Elizabeth had been uncertain, as they walked away from the house, leaving the cozy suburban landscape behind them and heading farther into the more rural areas, what her next move should be. While Josh kept an alert eye to any potential dangers, moving from walking in front of them to falling a few paces behind, he had not volunteered any further advice or suggestions after his original, shocking offer, and Elizabeth's mind felt like a blank slate. She could not think of anyone who could or would help them—if there was, in fact, anyone that she could turn to—and yet Maggie kept looking to her with a hopeful expression, assuming that her sister would do something now to put things right.

The weight of that expectation was almost too much, and Elizabeth wanted nothing more than to sit on the ground and cry. She had made the best plan she could, and it hadn't been enough, undone by Ray's willingness

to put other people into harm's way, to use vile tricks
and threats to get what he wanted. Meg had been her
best, nearest hope. The only other person she knew was
her father's uncle, an older man who lived out somewhere in Ohio. How were they supposed to get to Ohio,
and what was to stop Ray from sending his men there
first? Oh, God, what if he had already thought of that?
No. She would put no more people at risk. Whatever
they did, they would do themselves.

And that went for Josh's offer, too. His people
were already at risk. If Ray found them, he could—he
would—threaten to expose them, to turn them all into
the sideshow freaks she had taken Josh for, at first, if
they didn't hand Maggie over.

If Josh's herd was anything like Josh, they would
never let Maggie go into danger. Even if it put them in
danger, as well. She knew that the way she knew that
her arm was connected to her shoulder, or that Maggie
snorted when she was upset about something.

Everywhere she turned, it seemed as though things
just got worse, no matter what she did to solve the problems. She had the overwhelming urge to find a soft bed
somewhere and crawl under the covers. Then her brain
supplied the image—fueled by Josh's fresh scent next
to her, walking beside her—of not being alone in that
bed. Soft pillows and cool sheets and the warm flesh of
Josh's arms around her, his chest pressed against hers,
their legs entangling, the smooth ignition of his lips and
tongue on hers. She didn't think of herself as sexual,

often, or even sensual; she missed the physical aspects of being in a relationship but she wasn't panting after every available male. In fact, since the flu struck, she hadn't really thought about it at all, she'd been so worn down with caring for others, and then worrying about Maggie. But since she woke up that morning and saw Josh standing there, watching her…

No. It had started before that. While she slept that night, on the pine-bough bed, and for the first time in months, had dreams that were pleasant, not distressing.

When Josh, in his other form, had stood watch over them, and kept them from harm.

Elizabeth knew that she was strong. She could take care of herself, and her sister, under normal circumstances. Being chased by a man who should have been protecting them, threatened with violence and…and God knew what? Those were not normal circumstances.

"I'm glad Maggie called you," she said suddenly.

Josh didn't ask her why she felt the need to say it now, merely put his arm around her shoulders, and pulled her close for a one-armed embrace. "So am I," he said.

Maggie, ahead of them, didn't look back, but Elizabeth suspected that her sister had a smile on her face, from the way her steps took on a sudden bounce.

They had left the suburban development behind a while back, and the road they were following now was almost deserted, with only the occasional car passing them by. They were half-hidden by the trees along the side, the greening branches casting a comforting shade over them, and the feel of Josh's arm casually resting on her shoulders made Elizabeth feel, for a moment, like three ordinary people out for an ordinary stroll on an ordinary day.

It was illusion, but for a few seconds, she relished it. Then the clanging of bells startled her, and Josh's arm slipped away as he strode forward, passing Maggie, to see what was happening.

Josh stopped and pointed ahead, where red-and-white painted gates were coming down across the road, lights flashing red. The clanging bells were coming from there, matched by a rumbling noise and then a whistle heralding a long freight train coming into sight up ahead and to their left, riding a previously unseen track. There were ten, maybe twenty cars, all different colors, with different logos on their sides, slowing as the train came to the crossing, then chugging to a halt. The bells stopped, although the lights were still flashing.

There were no cars on their side, and only a single sedan waiting on the other side of the barrier.

Josh reached back and grabbed their hands, startling them both as he tugged them into a run. "Come on," he said. "Hurry!"

And just like that, somehow, they were running across the road, down the line of boxlike railroad cars, and then he jumped up, catching the handle of one sliding door that was slightly ajar, pushing it open even as his other hand reached backward, coaxing them to follow him up.

Elizabeth had grabbed her sister by the waist, lifting her up so that Josh could take her. He caught her as though she weighed nothing, depositing her inside the railroad car, and then turned back to Elizabeth, still hanging from the door's handle. His pale hair was windblown, his eyes alight with laughter, and she felt as though she was suddenly seeing an entirely new side of him, or a new person altogether. How many forms did he have?

"Come on," he called to her. "Before the gate lifts and they start up again!"

Even as he said that, the gate started to clang, and the bar began to lift. The fear of being left behind gave Elizabeth the impetus to swallow hard and make a running leap, scrambling for his hand even as the train whistle sounded. The train jolted forward, and they were thrown together, staggering into the dark interior of the car. His hands went around her waist, and there was a long instant where all that existed for her was the feel of them together, pressed face-to-face, her legs straddling one of his as she tried to maintain her balance.

And then the instant was over, and she was moving away, aware that Maggie was watching every move they made a little too carefully.

There was a man sitting on an overturned crate at one end, but he and Josh sized each other up once and then the old man had nodded and gone back to whatever he was writing in his notebook. And then the train lurched forward again, and they were moving.

The car was half-filled with plastic crates the size of refrigerators, but the floor was surprisingly clean, and Maggie was already busy making a little nest of sorts in the far corner, pulling out her sweatshirt to have something to sit on. Elizabeth did the same, and leaned against one of the crates, letting out a sigh. After a minute, Maggie scooted over and rested against her.

For the moment, at least, they could stop and relax, letting the rail rumble underneath them, taking them… somewhere else. No tickets, no map…no way to predict where they might get off or when. It was insane, and yet comforting, at the same time.

Maggie was too restless to stay still for long, and once the rocking of the car became more familiar, she got up to explore. Elizabeth was tempted to warn her to stay close, but Maggie skirted around the other man without being told, leaving him a full half of the car, and Josh was there watching, as well.

Reassured, Elizabeth took all three backpacks and resorted them so that they each had some food with them, just in case. Maggie had made very smart choices: except for the sandwiches she put out for them to eat now, it was all prepackaged goods that would keep—a small jar of peanut butter, a sleeve of crackers, a handful of granola bars and a box of pretzel sticks. She had also grabbed an assortment of fruit, including bananas, which Maggie hated—but knew that her sister loved. Touched, Elizabeth kept them for her own bag.

As she worked, she kept glancing up at Josh, who had settled on the floor across from her, and kept staring at the freight car's door with a strange, almost pained expression on his face. Once again she wondered what they were taking him away from—and why he was still traveling with them.

All at once he seemed to come to some decision, and when Maggie came back to them, he indicated that she should sit by him.

"I've not told you much about my family, have I?"

"You haven't told us anything," Maggie said, already anticipating a story.

"Ah. Well, we have the time now, don't we?"

Elizabeth kept working, but listened in, just as fascinated as her sister, as he began to spin patently fantastic tales of a great herd of Mustang, who lived just like normal people most of their lives, holding down jobs and going to school—but twice a year gathered in a great herd out on the Western plains, and returned to their proper state, running wild with the wind.

"In the herd, the stallions are there to protect and defend and otherwise be useful," he was telling Maggie now, "but it's the females who make the decisions."

"Like Elizabeth!" Maggie crowed, and then looked guiltily at her sister. Pleased that Maggie had recovered some of her fun-loving spirit, where she had been so fierce before, Elizabeth just smiled and shook her head.

"Yes. Elizabeth would have made an excellent leader," Josh said, smiling up at her, and then added, "but she is far too young. The eldest mare is the one who leads us. When I left, Grace had been herd-leader for forty years. Nobody crosses her!"

Maggie's eyes were side. "Is she mean?"

He laughed, with a wince of memory. "She can get very angry if you cross her, but no, she's not mean. She's a lovely woman, actually. I miss her." He smiled. "She's my grandmother."

Elizabeth, watching the two of them together, was taken aback that this quietly handsome man, so good with her sister, was the same creature that killed a man in cold blood and—she had no doubt—would have killed the other two and Meg as well, had she allowed it.

It was antithetical to everything she believed, that violence was no answer, that discussion and negotiation were the way to solve every problem, and yet…she had to admit that there would have been no negotiating with those men, because there was no negotiating with Ray. You either agreed with him, or you were wrong, and if you were wrong then your voice was of no importance.

She found herself, perhaps inevitably, comparing Josh to Cody. Both good-looking, yes, although Cody had been darker, with snapping black eyes that seemed to laugh constantly. Josh was more serious—a man who had seen the world, while Cody, like her, had never gone far beyond the Community.

Cody, as much as she had loved him, had never been

strong. He had never needed to; his sweet manner made people want to make him happy, and so life had been easy for him. Until she had come to him with her fears, and it had all gone downhill, and ended with him hanging from a rope slung over a tree in his backyard.

The rush of guilt came just as fast and hard, but she didn't let it swamp her. She had to focus on the living, now.

Josh was strong, in both of his forms, and definitely stubborn. Nobody would force him to do anything he didn't choose to do. He was also violent, where Cody had never, to the best of her knowledge, lifted his voice in anger. He was an unknown, and the unknown could be terrifying—and dangerous. And yet her body reacted to Josh in a way that she had never felt with Cody, in all the years she had known him.

Elizabeth's innate honesty twisted in her, and she had to admit—to herself at least—that she had never reacted this way to anyone, not even men she'd found unbearably hot, physically. No other man had managed to make her throat close up and her stomach get flutters and her— She hesitated, even in her mind not sure how to describe it. "Her vagina" sounded too clinical, and all the other words were too rude, but the euphemisms she had read as a teenager were just silly. Whatever word used, the truth was that when he looked at her with those dark eyes, his lids half-hooded and his gaze intent, he didn't have to be touching her and she was still wet and ready for him, aching for the feel of him, his hands, his mouth and, yes, his cock inside her. She remembered the feeling of being astride his back, in his other form, and her cheeks flushed hotly. Suddenly she understood the eroticism of horseback riding, although she suspected that her feelings were slightly different than most.

It would have been enjoyable, those memories, and that sensation of being ready to burst into flames every time he even looked at her, if Josh hadn't made it quite clear from the start that he would only be interested in a virgin.

Elizabeth looked away, afraid her thoughts might show on her face. She had been a virgin once. It really hadn't been anything special—she certainly hadn't been a better person before she had sex, or any more loving, or kind, or…

Enough, she told herself. *Whatever his reasons, he has reasons. Don't unicorns and virgins go together, after all?* Maybe that was why…he and Maggie certainly fit together well, even though she didn't think he saw Maggie as anything other than a little sister, now. The girl who talked to animals, and their self-appointed guardian who shifted into a unicorn at the first sign of trouble. It sounded like a fairy tale, a children's book. In this group, she was the odd one. The thought made her oddly melancholy. Her entire life, she thought she knew how life went, what her role was, who her friends were. One turn or twist of fate, and all that was revealed as a lie. Cody gone, Ray a danger, Elders coming after them rather than defending them, and Meg betraying them like that.

In the crucible of the bad things that had happened, Elizabeth had redefined herself, stripping away everything else—daughter, friend, baker, Community member—until only one role was left. Her only focus, for months now, had been protecting Maggie. With Josh— the Mustang—here now, sworn to protect her sister, what role could she, Elizabeth, play?

That melancholy thought occupied her while the train rattled on, and Josh told Maggie more and more outrageous stories about places he had been, and things he had seen, until the man at the other end of the car slapped his palm flat against the floor of the car, and they all jumped. Some sort of information seemed to pass between him and Josh, and when the man gathered up his belongings and slipped out the door—even though the train was still rolling, making Elizabeth gasp—Josh started to gather their own things, as well.

"We need to get out, now."

Elizabeth shook her head in protest. "But the train's still moving!"

"It will slow down soon, and then I'll want you to toss your bags out, and jump. I'll go first and be there for you, okay?"

Maggie was already grabbing her bag, making sure that her sneakers were tied tightly. She would fling herself out of a plane in midair, if her unicorn told her to.

"But why?" Elizabeth needed more than his say-so.

He hesitated, as though thinking over how much to tell her, how quickly. "We're coming to an area where they check the cars. We don't want to get caught."

"That man told you that?"

"There's an entire language for people who ride the rails, slang and hand symbols and markings. I don't know much of it, but there are a few signals I've learned."

An entire world Elizabeth couldn't even imagine, riding the rails, traveling like this on a regular basis. The Community, her home, her bakery, it all seemed another lifetime ago.

"Come on," he said, and Maggie went to the door, looking back over her shoulder as though asking the adults what was taking so long.

Josh moved to the door beside her and slid it open a little more. They were passing through farmland now, acres of green and brown, dotted with the occasional farmhouse and cut by single-lane roads. She looked down at the slope leading from the tracks, and the ground looked frighteningly faraway. There was no way Maggie could jump it, and the car showed no sign of slowing down, despite Josh's promises.

He saw their expressions, and seemed to debate something with himself, then nodded. "All right. We'll do this a different way. Get your packs on your back, and make sure they're secured, okay?" He handed his own pack to Elizabeth, and stepped away from them, back into the car.

And, like magic, he shifted. It couldn't have been more than a minute, and Elizabeth wasn't sure if she had actually seen his muscles stretch and elongate, his skin turning to hide, or if her brain just filled in those details to cover something even more impossible, but where Josh had stood, now the Mustang waited for them. A horse didn't have expressions, but she swore that he had the most impatient look on his...face? Muzzle? His eyes, that was it. No matter what his shape, those brown eyes were the same. It was almost enough to make her laugh, how splendid that realization was.

He struck one hoof against the floor, and lowered his proud neck, indicated that they should get a move on, and mount.

Maggie scrambled on first, her pack bobbing awkwardly over her shoulder as she put her foot into the cup of Elizabeth's hands and hauled herself onto that broad back. Once she was secure, she leaned forward, giving her sister room to mount, as well.

Elizabeth hesitated, the awareness that it was Josh inside that equine frame making her suddenly self-conscious. Reaching up to grab a handful of the thick white-blond mane that felt so similar to—and so un-like—Josh's hair, she leaned against his muscled neck and whispered an apology for pulling, then hauled herself up. Her right leg swung across his back and she settled herself behind Maggie, her free arm snaking around her sister's waist, both of them leaning forward to keep their balance, fingers tangled in his mane. Josh's knapsack was slung across her shoulder, opposite her own: an awkward solution, but she didn't know what else to do with it.

"All right," she said into one backward-pointing white ear. "As ready as we're going to get."

The Mustang walked to the now-open door, letting them settle onto his back as needed, and then paused. The train let out a long whistle, and the cars began to slow. Not enough, Elizabeth thought, gripping the mane tighter, closing her arms around Maggie as though that would keep her safe. Not nearly enough.

"We trust you," she heard her sister whisper into those white ears, and they flicked back once in acknowledgement, and then he gathered himself, and suddenly, awesomely, they were *flying*.

And before she could really appreciate it, or realize how terrified she was, or enjoy Maggie's delighted squeal, they landed hard on the ground, the impact jostling her bones and almost knocking them off the Mustang's back. He recovered almost immediately, racing away from the tracks with long strides that felt more comfortable than the rocking of the train.

They were in farmland for certain now, and she noted, even as the wind made her eyes tear, that he avoided stepping onto tilled ground, instead staying on the lumpier, less even land. The human brain inside the animal form, making sure that he didn't ruin anyone's crops.

The Mustang could be violent, yes. It could also be

gentle. She pulled her arm tighter around Maggie, making her sister mutter in protest, and let herself just enjoy the feel of so much horsepower underneath them, confident that he would not stumble, or let them fall.

Finally, his strides slowed to a walk and, his sides heaving slightly, he stopped, allowing them to slide off and rely on their own slightly wobbly legs.

"Oh, that was fun!" Maggie said in delight, and then stopped, her eyes going wide not with excitement, but fear. She looked over her shoulder, and then turned in a circle as though trying to catch a scent. Mustang, alerted by her behavior, or perhaps sensing something wrong on his own, mirrored her stance, turning slightly, preparing himself for action. His hooves struck at the ground, pawing at it.

"Baby? What is it?" Elizabeth asked.

"Bad animals," Maggie whispered, taking her sister's hand in her own cold one, all joy and laughter gone. "They found us."

Chapter 11

Her sister's words sent shock and fear back into Elizabeth as well, and the sense of foreboding and dread that had filled her dreams for so many weeks came flooding back in, raising all the doubts and fears that the Mustang's presence had driven away. Suddenly it didn't matter how brave they were, how sharp and strong his blows might be, if these "bad animals" could find them where they went, or what they did.

Maggie's scared expression kept her from saying or showing any of that. Instead, she tried to mimic Mustang's ready stance, as best her weaker human form could. It was difficult to prepare herself, though, not knowing what to expect. What were the bad animals? Neither sister's sense of them had been specific. Should they look for a wave of rabid dogs streaming toward them? A pride of lions, intent on the kill? A flock of birds, à la Hitchcock?

What they got was the nearby slam of a car door, and five figures walking toward them at a steady but unthreatening pace.

The ordinariness of it should have relieved Elizabeth. Instead, it made her tense even more. Another batch of Ray's goons, it had to be. It seemed almost anticlimactic after Maggie's pronouncement, but Elizabeth did not for a moment underestimate how dangerous this could get. Unlike the flea market, or Meg's suburban neighborhood, there was nobody out here to see what happened—nobody to stop them from using even more violence. Could Mustang's solid flesh deflect bullets? She didn't think so.

Elizabeth reached toward the unicorn's neck, intending to tell Maggie to get on and ride the hell away, but he shied away from her touch and she looked to him in astonishment.

His eyes were wide, his ears pricked forward, and his black-rimmed nostrils were flaring heavily, as though he were badly winded. If he were an ordinary horse she would have said he was about to bolt, but this was no ordinary horse. This was a Mustang. She reached out again and this time he let her place her hand against his side. The flesh was warm from their run, and she could feel his great heart pounding in his rib cage. Not from exertion, though. This was fear, yes, but also anger. She could feel the difference, touching him.

Bad animals. Whatever Maggie meant by that, whoever these people were, they frightened him, and his fear made him want to strike out, not run. Why was he frightened now, when before he had been so fierce?

"Bad animals," Maggie said in a whisper, pressing herself against Elizabeth's side and sliding an arm around her waist, hugging herself against her sister's body as though to disappear into her.

Looking back at the five figures, now much closer, Elizabeth saw that there was something...odd about three of them. They walked wrong—upright, but barely, with a rolling pace that was more akin to a giraffe's lope than a human's walk. Their bodies were out of proportion, or oddly elongated, and the way they held their heads, down and forward, not erect... Something prickled at the back of her neck, and she started to understand Mustang's fear.

Whatever was coming toward them...wasn't human. *Bad animals.*

"What do we do?" she asked the Mustang, who snorted once, roughly, and lowered his head so that his horn was pointing at a downward angle, at the intruders.

"Fight them? But how? We can't..."

The answer came to her as clearly as he'd spoken in her ear. They couldn't. He could.

"He wants us to hide," Maggie said.

"But..." Elizabeth looked around, uncomfortable

taking her eyes off the approaching creatures. They were in the middle of a field, in the middle of nowhere. How could they escape?

"The tree, over there," Maggie said suddenly. "We need to climb the tree."

Mustang snorted again, this time in approval, his own gaze never leaving the strangers. The two more human-moving forms had dropped back, while the other three moved forward. The oddness of their forms was more obvious now, and one of them dropped into a crouch in order to move forward more swiftly, not even bothering to mock human movement any longer.

"Libby, come on!" Maggie cried, pulling at her arm.

Her feet felt as though they were glued to the dirt, her legs stiff as boards. She didn't want to go. She didn't want to leave the Mustang, not to face these things alone.

"We'll only get in the way," Maggie said, reading her thoughts. "Run!"

Giving in, Elizabeth turned and ran.

The tree Maggie had pointed to was an old apple tree, tall and burly, with low enough branches that Elizabeth was able to boost Maggie up into one, and then reach up and swing herself onto another. Maggie was already scrambling higher, up into the leafier region, where she was less visible from the ground. Elizabeth, less certain that the boughs would hold her weight, stayed lower. From there, she would be able to see what happened, when monsters and unicorn met.

The thought made her heart race even faster than the sprint up into the tree had caused. They had left him there, alone, against three…whatever they were. Part of her wanted to look away, to cover her eyes and hide and pretend that none of it was real, none of it was happening, that she would close her eyes and wake up in her own bed, and the world would be right side up and normal again, her parents alive and Maggie just a normal girl nobody would look twice at.

Part of her couldn't look away.

They had left him there. Why had they left him there? Why didn't he run?

From her vantage point, she could see the creatures more clearly, and almost wished she couldn't. The foremost creature had a body that was long and lean and covered in a short black pelt, its face flattened like a cat's, but with human eyes and nose, and clawed hands instead of paws, like someone had twisted a leopard into a parody of human form. The two on either side were heavier, more grossly covered in thick, shaggy gray hair, and they had a more ponderous walk—but again, their faces were human. That was the part that made Elizabeth feel ill—not the animal part, but the impossible yet unmistakable humanity of them.

They were not bad animals. They were monsters. Even from here she could sense the wrongness, the anger and bitter viciousness of them.

And, with a sudden wash of nausea, she identified

them as the creatures from her dreams. This was what it had been warning her about.

Above her, Maggie whimpered. "Those things… they're pawing at me, in my head. They want to touch me…."

The monsters had stopped and were sniffing at the air, heads raised, and clearly looking for something. With a sinking feeling in her stomach, Elizabeth knew exactly what they were searching for, what they had wanted all along. She forced herself not to look up into the branches, not to do anything that might give her sister's location away. "Don't think about them," she whispered. "Just shut down and don't think at all, Maggie."

Hoping that her sister could do that, she forced herself to look away from the beasts, their hypnotic hideousness, and back to the Mustang, standing between the monsters and them. His legs were sturdy and square on the ground, his head still lowered, the horn glinting as though from within, a not-so-subtle threat. His white hide and straw-gold mane and tail sparkled in the sun, and the black of his hooves seemed even darker as he pawed once against the grass and snorted in challenge. Other than that sound, the day was utterly silent. The three creatures, now paused a few yards away, did not make a noise, and even the birds and insects had ceased, the wind carrying not a hint of noise from the now-distant road. The entire world might have gone still for this battle.

The weight of it overwhelmed her, until she wanted

to scream, to shakes the braches around her, just to make something happen.

And then something did. Without warning, the cat-creature leaped forward, directly at Mustang, clearly planning to bypass the lowered head and land on his back. The speed and ferocity of the attack shook a noise from Elizabeth, although it was a muted scream, stifled by one hand clamped over her mouth even as the other kept a firm grip on her branch.

The monster's hands might be human but the claws that flashed down on his neck were pure feline: sharp and vicious. Mustang swerved, but couldn't quite avoid the swipe. Three lines of red showed clearly against that white flesh, and Elizabeth shoved the heel of her hand into her mouth to keep from making another sound in response. He had to keep all his attention on the battle, and not be worrying about them.

She risked a look upward, to check on Maggie. Her sister had reached the next-higher branches, and was huddled against the trunk, her face hidden from the scene below. There was a flicker of gray; a squirrel, come down to sit on her shoulder, its little paws clinging to her shirt as though to give comfort, and the thought, somehow, settled Elizabeth's fears enough to let her look down again at the battle below them.

The cat-thing spun, and the two of them engaged in a terrible, silent dance, back and forth, the monster ducking under Mustang's hooves, while he kept his body outside the reach of those claws, dashing and swerving on the grass. He kept trying to get at the beast with his horn, but it clearly knew the danger, and curved its body each time to avoid impact.

Meanwhile, the two more brutish beasts had taken up position on either side, and were closing in, moving with slow, heavy steps. Their arms lifted, showing claws that were even longer and thicker than the cat-thing's; weapons that were meant to rend flesh apart, not merely scratch. Even as Elizabeth worked her mouth to yell a warning, Mustang reacted, ducking backward with a short burst of elegant speed, slipping out of their trap with bare seconds to miss, and then charging forward again as they turned to face him. He reared up, exposing his undefended stomach for a heartbeat too long, while Elizabeth's heart skipped a beat, and then he slashed down with his tar-black hooves.

There was a cracking noise that Elizabeth could hear even in the tree, and the left-side beast howled in pain, grabbing at its arm and swinging its body madly, like a child having a temper tantrum. Mustang didn't pause, but lowered his head and rammed forward, not at the downed monster, but the cat-beast now behind it.

The remaining bear-beast attacked again, scoring another swipe on Mustang's hindquarters as he went past, but the unicorn was too swift for it. The bear-beast lifted its blocky head and bellowed, a terrible noise like a broken church bell. In response, the first monster got to its feet, one arm still wrapped around its injuries, and tried to grab at Mustang's tail as he went past.

In the noise and confusion, Mustang still managed to get at the cat-beast with the tip of his horn, and the thing sprang back with a scream that made all the hair on Elizabeth's arms shiver, and her teeth clench in reaction. It was the cry of something in mortal agony, unbearable pain, as though someone had thrown acid into its eyes. Even hating and fearing the thing as much as she did, Elizabeth felt an instant pang of sympathy. Nothing should ever be in that much pain.

Mustang drove forward again, nicking the cat-beast again, and it dropped to all fours in an attempt to make a smaller target, crouching and snarling at him in defiance.

"The horn's an antidote to poison." Maggie's voice floated down, a soft, scared whisper. "All the stories say that. A unicorn's horn can cure anything."

So, against something this twisted—could it drive the monsters away? Elizabeth barely dared hope. The injured bear-beast was up on its feet again, moving forward at a steady, if shuffling, pace. Mustang, his head still down to hold the cat-beast at bay, somehow kicked backward with his hind legs, his entire body straightening out in the kick. He made contact, his hooves knocking the bear-beast in the face and sending it staggering back with another howl of pain. There was no time to celebrate, though, as Elizabeth saw the uninjured bear-creature rush into the fray again, coming at Mustang from his blind side. It had picked up a stick somewhere, and swung it, landing a heavy blow against the Mustang's neck. The branch shattered, but the impact made Mustang stagger slightly. When that happened, the horn lost its contact on the cat-beast, allowing it to scramble away. It moved much more slowly, though, indicating that the horn had caused a great deal of damage.

The bear-creature tried to rush him again, this time without the stick. His attention seemingly on the injured cat-beast, Mustang did a move that Elizabeth could barely follow, much less explain. He seemed to almost lift himself into the air, a graceful leap straight up, rising out of reach for half an impossible second, at the same time he was executing a double-leg kick that sent the bear-beast flying back, out of striking range. And then, without visible effort, the Mustang twisted in the air, his body almost folding on itself, so that he came down facing the opposite direction, ready to continue battle.

Elizabeth's heart wrenched at the beauty of the move, even as her gut clenched at the blood splattered over his hooves and legs, staining the white.

The cat tried to escape, and was dealt a sideways kick that left its ribs crushed in, even as Mustang's head lowered and he went after the uninjured bear-beast. Trying to grab at the Mustang's head left the bear's upper body exposed, and too close; the horn stabbed directly through its chest. The beast staggered and then fell back, sliding off the horn.

An almost puzzled hesitation crossed its ursine face, as though it was trying to figure out what had just happened, and it fell over backward, sitting down hard on the ground and then slumping over to its side. It didn't move again.

The other bear-thing took one look at its companions and, howling in fear or pain, turned to run back to the two humans who were still watching. It had barely made it halfway back when there was a loud crack, and it, too, fell over, groping at its side.

Meanwhile, Mustang staggered, his hind leg giving slightly. The cat-thing snarled once at him, defiantly aggressive even in its own pain, until the Mustang stabbed at it again with his horn. The beast tried to lash out, but faltered, and then lay still, blood flowing from its wounds down into the muddy ground.

"They shot their own creature?" Maggie asked from her perch above, horrified. "But…"

"No buts, come on," Elizabeth cried, and started to scramble down the tree. She didn't care that the beasts were still there, or that the humans apparently had guns. Mustang was hurt, and needed help.

Mustang must have heard them, because his head turned, and the glare he sent said as clearly as words: *stay put.* Then he turned and, ignoring his own wounds, leaped over the still body of the cat-beast, and raced forward, heading straight for the humans.

"They'll shoot him!" Maggie cried, her voice cracking in fear.

"Maggie!" Elizabeth was struck by a sudden inspiration. "He's scaring them. They're going to be scared!"

Her sister gaped at her for a moment, unable to comprehend what Elizabeth was telling her. "But…"

Elizabeth stared up at her sister still hidden in the tree, at the squirrel sitting on her shoulder, willing her to understand. She didn't have time to be gentle, or kind, or consider the ramifications of what she was about to tell her sister to do. "He needs you to distract them, Maggie! You have to do it! Do it!"

Years of training, of reassurances and lessons, undone by those two words. Elizabeth felt ill, but she'd had no other choice.

Maggie set her jaw, and her eyes took the faraway glaze that meant that she was reaching out. But not to animals this time. Not to anything so innocent. The squirrel let out an odd noise, and leaped from her shoulder, disappearing into the branches far above. Maggie didn't even notice. She shuddered once, as though feeling those unnatural minds reaching for her again, and then let out a tiny gasp of air.

"Scared," she said softly, barely loud of enough for Elizabeth to catch. "So scared. You should be scared. He's so much better than you are, stronger and faster and smarter and *better* and… You. Should. Run."

It was against everything they had told her was good, and right. Her parents, good, kind, gentle people, would have been horrified.

Her parents had not seen what their daughters had seen. Elizabeth discovered that she felt only a minor pang of guilt at telling Maggie to turn her skills on people deliberately. Especially when the two figures dropped their weapons and bolted for the safety of their vehicle, Mustang still bearing down hard on them. He swerved just before they started the engine, disappearing into a half-grown cornfield, even though the stalks were barely shoulder-high and he should have been plainly visible.

"Like magic," Elizabeth said, even though she was sure he had probably just knelt down or something, to go out of sight.

Or changed. Something in her bones told her that Mustang had shifted back to Josh, and every instinct she had was to go to him, hurt and bleeding and all their fault, but she couldn't go not yet. Not until…

The driver decided against driving into the cornfield, or getting out himself to investigate, and instead put the vehicle into Drive, coming closer to where the two girls were hiding. Elizabeth scrambled back up into the tree, scraping the skin in her hands and arms as she did so, thankful for Josh's choice of dark colors for them, which would not stand out from within the leafy confines of the tree. So long as they stayed still, and quiet, and did not move, they should be safe.

Should be.

The sound of the car came closer, far too close, and they huddled against the tree trunk, trying to be as invisible as possible, not daring to climb back higher or deeper into the branches for fear of that movement being spotted.

The vehicle stopped, nowhere near their tree, and two figures got out. This close, Elizabeth could see that the car was actually one of the miniature trucks Elizabeth would see out in the fields sometimes, near the Community. An agro-truck, her father had called them.

A man and a woman got out, the same two figures who had let loose the monsters, and Elizabeth stifled a gasp. The woman she didn't know, but the man was the same one who had been at Meg's house earlier, who had tried to take Maggie. Who had tried to hurt Maggie.

One thought swept away all others on a wave of dark red rage: she should have let Mustang kill them, then.

"Hurry," the woman said, her voice harsh and worried-sounding. "I'll be damned if I wait around here, with that thing still unaccounted for." She turned to look back toward the cornfield, as though expecting the Mustang to come back out, three times as high and breathing flame. Elizabeth noticed the glint of metal in the woman's hand, and sent a silent message to Josh, the same one he had sent to them: *stay put. Don't move.*

Resting her face against the rough bark of the tree trunk, feeling it dig into her flesh as a way to concentrate on anything other than what might be happening in that cornfield, Elizabeth waited while the two figures loaded the bodies of the dead beasts into the back of the truck without ceremony. They threw a tarp over the evidence, and then drove off across the field, heading for the road. Only then did Elizabeth let the inevitable conclusion sink in to her conscious mind. The truck, those people, the sense of those monsters that had first made her uneasy, back in the bakery? All meant one thing.

The "bad animals" had come from the Community.

Surrounded by tall stalks of corn, Josh lay on his side, panting with the effort of trying to control the pain. The ground was hard and surprisingly cold, and there were dry sticks digging into his side. His clothing was damp with sweat and blood, not all of it his, but enough to worry him.

If the beasts followed him, they would be able to track him by scent alone. Had he left any alive to follow? He couldn't remember. Normally his memory was sharp no matter what form he was in; his mind remained much the same as Josh or Mustang. But he couldn't think, couldn't focus. The cat's snarls, the sting of claws, the hairy arm coming down on him from behind, the overwhelming feeling of fear not for himself but for others....

Elizabeth. And Maggie. Were they safe? They had gone up a tree. But they had come down again. He remembered that, remembered seeing Elizabeth starting toward him, concern written on her lovely face, those expressive eyes, and he had warned her to stay put... hadn't he? He thought he had shouted, but of course he couldn't, not in Mustang form.

Were they safe? It was the dominant question in his mind now, shutting out even the pain in his ribs and the queasy sensation in his stomach, and the worry that someone might be searching for him, ready to bring down a club or claw and snuff out the last bit of daylight. If the girls were safe, he could accept that. If only he knew they were safe....

There was a rustling in the plants, somewhere behind him, and Josh's fingers closed in the dirt, trying to find something, anything that could be used as a weapon. But there was only loam and weeds, and the effort used up the last of his strength.

"I'm sorry," he whispered. "I tried..."

"Oh, my God."

Elizabeth's voice, filled with soft horror. At him?

"Maggie," he managed to say. "Is she all right?"

"She's fine." Elizabeth knelt next to him, her newly shortened hair falling in her face. He wanted to see that sweet mouth, to touch it one last time.

"Don't be an idiot," she said, and he realized he had vocalized that last bit. He was confused again...he could speak? He was in human form. He had shifted back. In Mustang form he could think whatever he wanted and it couldn't be spoken, but he rarely spoke in human form when he was away from his people, preferring to watch and listen rather than participate. He had told stories to Maggie, sitting there in the train car, so he wouldn't blurt what was in his head to Elizabeth.

Safer to be in Mustang form. But he could not find the energy to shift.

The rut, absent for long enough that its return was almost a shock, rose in him again as her hand touched his face. She lingered there, gently, and then moved down his torso, lightly touching his skin, searching for injuries, unaware of the pain she was causing him with that touch.

The rut sparked and surged, filling his cock with blood and his veins with fire. If he had the strength he would have rolled her over onto the ground, covered her body with his own, ground dirt into their skin as they made love in the cornfield, the sky spread out blue above them, the smell of honey in the air and the sound of birds around them.

The smell of honey was Elizabeth, he decided, and hoped that he hadn't said that out loud, too.

"You're hurt. I don't know if I can move you… Maggie!" she called over her shoulder. "Get the first-aid kit from my bag!"

Of course she had a first-aid kit. His Elizabeth was always prepared.

Maggie came through the stalks and knelt beside him as well, her dark eyes as worried as her sister's. There were leaves and twigs tangled in her braids, pulling strands of hair out of the once neat plaits, and a streak of mud across one high cheekbone. "Is he gonna die?"

Yes, he tried to tell her. *I'm sorry.*

"No." Elizabeth was definite. "But he's pretty banged up. I need to stop the bleeding." She opened the kit and took out a sterile gauze pad, tape and a pair of tiny scissors. "Now we'll see how useful that Girl Scout badge was," she said. "Brace yourself, Josh. This is probably going to hurt."

She put one gentle hand on his shoulder, and with the other, pulled the bloodied cloth away from his skin.

His teeth clenched, and the world swam. When he was able to focus again, his shirt was in shreds on the ground next to him, and there was a clean white bandage on his side. The tape felt oddly cold.

"I think you've got at least one cracked rib, and a concussion," she told him softly. "And there may be internal bleeding, things I can't see or deal with. But we have to get out of here. We— You and Maggie sent them running, but if they come back with more of those… things…" She shuddered, and Josh found the energy to reach his arm up, to capture her face in one hand and coax her down so that he could kiss those lips again.

Honey. Definitely honey. Alfalfa honey.

She let him kiss her, her own lips softening under the touch, heedless of her sister beside them, but then pulled back. Exhausted, he let her.

"Can you stand?"

He couldn't, but he would try. Because the alternative was to stay here, and to stay was to die. Every instinct he had agreed with her on that.

"Will it be easier for you, in your other form?"

He considered that, staring up at the blue sky overhead, and forced his voice to work consciously.

"Maybe. Not sure I can shift, though. Too tired."

"Damn it. I can't carry you. Not without making things worse."

"Tell him to shift."

"What?"

Josh blinked up at Maggie, who was staring at him intently. Her eyes were telling him something, but he couldn't hear her. She could only call him when he was in Mustang form.

"Tell him to shift. He has to listen to you. You're the lead mare."

Elizabeth looked at her sister as though she had lost her mind, and then gave a shrug as though to say *what could it hurt.* "Josh, we need you to shift to your other form. It's the only way to get you to safety."

He heard her, but still couldn't bring himself to do more than pull up his legs, as though getting ready to stand up.

"You have to boss him around," Maggie said, her voice urgent.

"Josh. You will shift!"

Her voice wavered, but there was enough there to move him. Maggie was right. She was the eldest female, the wisest of them, even if she wasn't Mustang, and so he obeyed. Muscles melted and flexed, the strange ebb and tide of blood and bone that came with every shift, and he was scrambling to his feet, swaying a little as he did so. The scent of the monsters came back to him, and he tried to go on alert, to protect his herd, but he did not have the strength to fight again.

Warm hands touched his neck and hindquarters, and his skin shuddered in pleasure at the touch, the rut mingling with something else, smoothing it out into a pleasurable burn. These were hands he knew. They were loving hands, healing hands, and he let them guide him, his head hung low with exhaustion, out of the cornfield and back into the open.

The bodies were gone. He could smell their foul taint lingering in the air, see the depression in the grass where he had fought them, smell the blood—human-not-human blood—staining the grass, but they were gone. His senses told the story of what he had missed: a vehicle had driven up, stopping there, and humans had taken the bodies away.

"Come on," Elizabeth urged him, her hand still on his neck. "Come on. This way. There's a farmhouse a little way down, Maggie says. We can get help there."

No. It was too dangerous. He could not let them go into danger.

But his legs, moved by instinct, followed her even as his mind argued. She was lead mare. He would follow her anywhere.

Chapter 12

Not far from where he had fought the beasts, there was a wide graveled road, thankfully empty of any traffic. The three of them staggered down the slight slope onto it, and headed the way Maggie had said they should go. He didn't know how she knew—maybe she had sensed domesticated animals there? But the teenager seemed certain, dashing from his side to run ahead a few yards, then coming back like an overexcited puppy.

The Mustang could feel his body shaking more with every step, until he was leaning as much on Elizabeth as he dared without knocking her over. Unlike Maggie, she was a steady presence at his side. Her hand stayed on his neck, and her soft voice murmured nonsense into his ear, keeping his mind focused on her. The rut had faded under the mutual onslaught of physical pain and her comfort, and his body kept moving forward to follow her lead. He could only manage a slow, plodding walk, but it covered the ground at a pace Elizabeth could match without trouble.

When they came to a sturdy-looking fence, clearly meant to keep livestock in rather than intruders out, surrounding a small farm with a large, neat-looking barn and a house with white siding and blue shutters, she told him that it was all right to shift back now.

The moment he was back in human shape, he collapsed, and only Elizabeth's quick hands saved him from going face-first into the dirt. She eased him to the ground, leaning him against a fencepost. The wood scratched uncomfortably against his bare back, but sitting down felt so good, he almost didn't mind.

"Ribs...definitely broken," he said.

"Yeah." She sat next to him, her hand taking his own and holding it gently.

"Josh?" Maggie came racing back to them, her pretty features scrunched up in worry.

"Go run on ahead, baby," Elizabeth told her. "See if anybody's home up there. We're going to need some help getting him the rest of the way."

She nodded, and turned to run through the gate and up the drive to the house.

"I actually feel better," Josh said, while they waited for Maggie to return.

"Liar," she said, squeezing his hand.

He did feel better, though. Her presence soothed him, although the physical wounds were severe and he would have gone face-first to plead for painkillers, if there were any available. Even his near-constant erection was less of a demand and more of a promise, although he couldn't let himself think of that. In the shape he was in right now, just kissing Elizabeth would kill him. Didn't mean he couldn't close his eyes and imagine it, though.

The farmhouse was owned by a middle-aged couple who apparently took one look at Maggie, muddy and bedraggled, and melted. Twenty minutes after she had run off, an old Jeep drove up to them, and Maggie and a bulky, balding man got out, leaving the door ajar in his hurry.

"Oh, the poor thing, you poor things," the man said. "Lou," he called back to the Jeep's driver, "get the medical kit out of the back." He knelt down next to Josh, across from Elizabeth, and took a small penlight out of his pocket. "It's all right, boy. I'm vet-trained, but I did some medic work back when. You're in good hands until we can get you to the hospital."

The idea of a vet coming to his rescue amused Josh, and he managed not to flinch when the man shone his light into his eyes.

"Good response," he said. "Good. Has he been unconscious at all since the beating?"

Elizabeth shot a glance at Maggie, as though to ask what story she had told them, then shook her head. "No. He's been groggy, but awake the whole time."

"Good, good. You did this bandaging? Good work. I won't disturb that 'til we have him back in the house. Nasty bruise, that, and these cuts, those are nasty. What did they hit you with?"

"A pitchfork," Elizabeth said quickly. "They swung it at him, and he couldn't get out of the way soon enough."

"Will be a tetanus shot for you then, boy. Come on, carefully now. Lou, you drive home, while this young lady and I handle the boy in back. You, missy, ride in front with Lou. And drive slow, you!"

His partner, a shorter, dark-haired man with deep laugh lines around his mouth and eyes, looked heavenward as though asking for patience, and then shooed Maggie back into the Jeep ahead of the others.

The trip back was as gentle as Lou could make it, but Elizabeth felt every jolt and jounce in the road, and could only imagine how bad it was for Josh. He lay in the back of the Jeep, his legs on her lap, while the doctor—Kit, he said his name was—tended to the lacerations. It was crowded in the backseat, but the older man's hands were steady and sure, and Elizabeth whispered a tiny prayer of thanks to whoever might be listening that, of all the houses they might have come to, they had chosen this one. At the same time, she was aware that they couldn't stay too long; she would not bring trouble to these people, for the crime of kindness.

"What did you tell them?" she asked her sister in a low whisper.

"Bad men," Maggie whispered back in a sad, quivering voice. "My sister and her boyfriend and I were hiking, and bad men came and beat him up."

Well, it had the virtue of being far more plausible than the truth, and had certainly done the job. The couple seemed personally affronted by Josh's wounds.

At the house, Kit half carried Josh inside, his bulky frame handling the younger man's form without any obvious difficulty.

"You girls go in and wash up," Lou directed them, as he picked up the medical kit and ushered them inside. "Bathroom's that way, just inside the door. Don't you worry, if Kit needs help he'll call, but I'm betting your friend won't want witnesses when he's in pain. God forbid we see them as mere mortals." One of his bright brown eyes dropped a wink, and despite her exhaustion and worry, Elizabeth felt herself smiling at him in response. "And we'll have him fixed up just fine, don't worry. Kit knows what he's doing.

"And we're quite well guarded here. Nobody will get in as we don't allow it."

Maggie, ahead of them on the steps, stumbled a little at that, then recovered and went inside, but Lou had noted that, too. Elizabeth was starting to think that there wasn't much he didn't see.

"Kit and me, we won't ask you questions," Lou said quietly, adult-to-adult. "Some things we don't want to know. It's enough you're in need of help, and that we can offer it."

"Thank you."

"Go, girl. Wash. I'll see if I can't find you a new sweatshirt—that one's all over in dirt."

Fifteen minutes later, her face and hands had been scrubbed until the last of the dirt and blood was gone, and she was clad in a mint-green cotton T-shirt in place of her muddy, bloody top. There was an oversized mug of tea waiting on the kitchen counter when she emerged, while Lou ran a brush through Maggie's unbraided hair, picking the leaves and twigs out with a distracted tsking, the way one might groom a dog. Maggie, her lap full of squirming kittens, seemed perfectly content.

"Now there's a homey sight," Kit said from the doorway. He wore a dark blue lab smock over his clothing, and wiped his hands on a towel. "Your man's asleep," he said to Elizabeth before she could even ask. "With luck he'll stay that way for a few hours. The scratches were bad but treatable, and there was only one cracked rib. No other damage that I could find."

Elizabeth stared at him, not sure if she should be pleased or disbelieving. She had seen the damage. She had felt the blood flowing out of his body, heard the crunch of bones when he tried to move. How…

A calico kitten escaped from Maggie's lap, stalking over to its mother, who was grooming herself in the corner, seemingly unconcerned with the fact that her babies had been lap-napped. Maggie, under the guise of rearranging the remaining kittens, caught her sister's attention.

"Magic," Maggie mouthed, and Elizabeth nodded, reluctant but, finally, accepting. Magic. Impossible, and yet how much more impossible than a man who shifted his shape in the first place? How much more impossible than monsters with the forms of animals and the faces of humans? A girl who could call animals with her thoughts? If she was going to accept some of it, she had to accept all of it.

So far, she thought she was doing quite well on that front. No hysterics, no foolish and time-wasting denials.

But, someday soon, she was going to sit down and have a nervous breakdown.

"These men," Kit said, tossing the towel into a hamper and pulling off his smock to reveal jeans and an old shirt underneath. "You think they'll be coming back for a second round?"

Lou tsked disapprovingly at his partner, but he shook his head and waited for Elizabeth's answer.

"Most likely."

"Then we need to have you on your way before then" was all he said, as he sat down and picked up the newspaper.

And that, as far as Kit and Lou were concerned, was that. The girls were given a room with a twin bed that was piled high with comfortable-looking pillows, and covered by a quilt that had clearly been handmade.

"Shall we flip a coin for the bed?" Maggie asked, trying to be cheerful, but her expression didn't match the forced lightness of her words.

"I'll take the pillows, you keep the mattress," Elizabeth said. There was a thick rug on the floor; she suspected it would be more comfortable—and cleaner—than the mattress in the motel, if not the pine bower.

When they came downstairs, Kit reported that Josh was still sleeping, which was exactly what he needed in order to heal. Dinner was simple but filling, and the conversation skirted, as promised, around anything more weighty than the weather, the number and personalities of the kittens, and Maggie's least favorite topics in school. There was a pear cobbler for dessert, the adults had coffee and by the time the outside air had turned dark, Maggie was sleepy-eyed and yawning. Elizabeth sent her off to take a bath and go to bed.

When Elizabeth went up to say good-night, she was struck by how young and innocent Maggie looked, lying there, her hair dark against the white sheets, the pillows piled on the rug next to the bed.

"Baby, I'm sorry."

"It's okay," her sister said sleepily. "I'm all sorts of tired. I don't even think I'll notice there aren't any pillows."

"That wasn't what I meant."

"I know." Maggie yawned, her jaw practically cracking with the effort. "Go on, check on Josh. Tell him I said good-night, too."

When Elizabeth went back to the main room, Lou had settled on the sofa with a book, the lamplight picking out the silver in his brown hair, his face set in contented lines as he turned the page. Not wanting to disturb the other man, Elizabeth went quietly down the hallway to the room where Josh had been put.

Kit was there, putting away his stethoscope and looking slightly concerned but not worried.

"How is he doing?" Elizabeth asked softly.

"Better than he has any right to do," Kit told her. "I suspect he will be up and around in a few days, which considering the way his wounds looked just a few hours ago is quite remarkable. I've known a few fast healers in my years of practice, but whatever it is in his system, I'm tempted to bottle it and make myself a snake-oil fortune."

Elizabeth had a flash of concern—had the doctor somehow figured out that Josh wasn't what he seemed?—but no, Kit was taking it all at face value, that Josh had not been hurt as badly as first inspection suggested, and just recovered quickly.

Or, as Lou had said, they weren't the type to ask questions.

"Elizabeth."

Josh's voice was hoarse, and nowhere near as strong as it should have been, but it drew Elizabeth to the side of his bed like a steel cable. His skin was chalky, and there was a line of sweat on his forehead, plastering his hair to his scalp. She reached backward and pulled a straight-backed chair away from the wall, close enough to the bed that when she sat down, her left thigh was pressed against the mattress. "Hi, there," she said.

"I'll leave you two alone then," Kit said, already fading from Elizabeth's awareness. All that she could see was the sheen of pain in Josh's brown eyes, and the way that his fingers lay on the blanket, as though asking her to lace her own with them. So she did.

"Maggie found us a veterinarian," she told him lightly, watching as his pale fingers tightened around her own darker-skinned ones, and then looked back up to his face to see some of the lines on his face ease away at the contact.

"I've probably heard all the jokes already," he told her, but managed to smile. "I'll be all right. We heal quickly, my family."

Elizabeth smiled in return, but could feel the strain to hold it, and she was afraid it looked more like a grimace. "So I noticed. You might have mentioned that to me before I panicked, thinking you were going to die?"

"It was…a close thing. You saved my life, Elizabeth. If you hadn't found me then…"

"If it hadn't been for you, we would have been dead already," she replied, and was taken aback by the spasm of pain that crossed his face. "Are you all right, should I call Kit back?"

"No!" His fingers tightened more around hers, keeping her there when she would have gotten up, gone for help. "So long as you're here, I'm all right." There was an odd note in his voice, as though the fact shocked him. "I'm all right, so long as you're near me."

He drew a breath, carefully, as though testing his ribs, or what he was about to say was painful.

"I don't know how long it will last, though."

What would last? she wondered, totally confused by his words. Only the feel of his hand holding hers seemed real, at that moment, the heat of his skin touching hers. The rest of the world—the worries, the fears—receded into the foggy distance, even her sister.

Josh looked her in the eye, unflinching. "Elizabeth... I shouldn't be here. I'm supposed to be on search."

"Search?"

He nodded, not breaking eye contact. "I need...I need to find my mate."

Understanding broke over her, a cold shower of realization. "The pure virgin." She heard the bitterness in her voice; were they still so backward as a culture, to venerate a woman's virginity over anything else? Or was it just his culture, his people?

He heard the bitterness, too, and he looked away from her, instead gazing over her shoulder, as though seeing something in the distance, far away. "It's what we do. It's what we are. Unicorn and virgin. The myths were right about that, anyway. But I don't care. I...I don't understand it, but being next to you, being with you...it feels right. The rut fades, and the urge to search goes away, when you're next to me."

Now she was confused all over again. "You sound like that's a bad thing."

"It is." He refocused on her face, and hurried to explain. "Oh, God, no, Elizabeth, not because of you, don't take it that way, but...the rut is part of us, the males of the herd. It drives us, tells us when it's time to find a mate, to rejoin the herd. If we don't heed it..."

"What happens?" Her voice was steady, which surprised Elizabeth. She was feeling a lot of things right now, and not one of them was "steady." Confused, and worried, and, all right, more than a little fluttery inside because of the way his hand was still warm against hers, but... The worry won out. "Josh, what happens if you don't search, and find your virgin mate?"

He didn't want to tell her. She could tell that, and it made her all the more determined to get it out of him.

He closed his eyes, and tried to turn his head away, but Elizabeth used her free hand to cup his cheek so he couldn't look away.

"Tell me," she said, doing her best to make it a lead-mare command.

"If I don't satisfy the rut, I will be trapped in four-legged self for the rest of my life. I won't be able to shift any longer."

The words came out softly, and Elizabeth heard them, but it took a minute for her to understand.

"Trapped...in unicorn form?"

"Yes." He laughed, a tired chuckle, still not looking at her, but leaning into her touch. "I enjoy my four-legged form, and some of my kin choose to spend most of their lives that way, running with the wild horse herds we protect, but it wasn't how I had seen myself growing old. I wanted to be part of humanity as well as herd. I never really thought about what it would require, not until the rut came on me last week. And even then— I always planned to settle down and have children, so why not now? And if my instinct led me rather than my brain…was there really all that much difference? The couples in my herd, they're happy, they love each other. It works out the way it should.

"But I can't let you go, Elizabeth. I think about it, I tell myself I have to do it, and I can't. I can't turn away, go looking for someone else, not when you're next to me. No matter what the cost."

"Shhhh. Just…shhh. Stop it." Her mind was whirling, too much shoved at her all at once. Forever in horse form? Because of her? Her hand still on his face, her thumb stroked the soft skin under his eye, trying to soothe him. "How much time do you have? How… Josh, how much time did you waste, helping us?"

"Not a waste," he said, smiling a little, a hint of sweetness. "I have to make sure that you and Maggie are safe."

Suddenly she was angry—no, furious. "Not a waste? You risked your self…not just injury but forever… Are you an idiot?"

"Yes."

That soft admission broke her heart, and she leaned forward and rested her head against his shoulder, not caring how uncomfortable the position was for her, his fingers still twined with hers.

"Oh, Josh…"

"I told you. If you and Maggie are safe, it's all worth it." He tried to smile. "The fact that the rut is quiet when I'm with you, that has to mean something."

She couldn't scold him, not when he said things like that, but she had to be practical, pragmatic. Someone in this group had to be sensible! "Maybe it's Maggie. She's a virgin."

His chuckle rumbled under her touch. "Don't be an idiot. She's too young. It takes more than puberty to make a girl into a woman, and that's what the rut looks for."

"A suitable mate." And she, Elizabeth, wasn't suitable. But he wanted her…that was what he had said, wasn't it? This thing she felt, he felt it, too. But that didn't matter.

It hurt, stabbing hurt, to be told, however indirectly, that she wasn't suitable. The thought that he would leave her, go to another woman, be with that woman all his life, that another woman would have that place in his heart, in his home, in his bed… The thought was an emotional injury, an ice-pick stab from nowhere, hard and cold into her heart.

Elizabeth had been in love before, had lovers she had cared deeply about, and never before had the thought of being without one of them left her feeling like this, twisted and cold and aching inside her chest. She didn't like it, at all. Josh had somehow taken something from her, some freedom she'd had before, with his admission, and it made her want to get up and run out the door, to grab Maggie and flee....

"Don't leave me, Elizabeth. Please don't leave me."

The urge settled down, the coldness offset by the warmth of his hand, his voice. "I won't."

She wouldn't leave him, and not just because she felt guilty for his injuries, or that they needed him in order to avoid or run off Ray's men, to get Maggie somewhere safe. But she wouldn't let him sacrifice his future for them, either. No matter what he thought he felt, right now.

Josh was still trying to convince her that it was all right. "There's time, yet. The rut is just warning me that my days as a bachelor stallion are over, that's all. So long as I can still shift, still hold human form, it's okay. We'll have time to get Maggie somewhere safe, somewhere they can't reach her, somewhere protected."

"And then..." Elizabeth heard her voice break, and hated herself for it, for showing weakness when she needed to be strong. "And then we'll find you your mate."

Outside the door, unheard by either of them, Maggie rested her forehead against the door, hot tears in her eyes, and guilt in every inch of her frame. She hadn't wanted to eavesdrop; she had woken and wanted to make sure Josh was okay.

All this because she had called him. Because Ray

wanted her for something. Because she was different. Home lost, humanity lost, love lost…because of her.

No. Her mouth firmed into a hard line, and she moved away from the door. No. Maggie wasn't dumb; she knew what her sister had sacrificed to keep her safe, both when their parents died, and now.

It was her turn to be brave.

Josh tried to argue with her determination to find his missing mate, but Elizabeth held firm.

"You aren't going to be stuck anywhere because you helped us," she said. "You don't know how determined I can be, Mustang."

"Oh, I think I have some idea," he said, but his voice was drowsy, and whatever Kit had given him was starting to kick in.

Leaving Josh to get some rest, Elizabeth went back upstairs to the room she was sharing with her sister. It was a small attic space, barely even a bedroom, except for the narrow bed and wardrobe against one wall. They used it for when Kit's grandson came to visit, Lou had explained when he showed them the space. He was only ten, and spent more time outdoors than in, so they had never bothered to update the furnishings.

Elizabeth had assured Lou that they were thankful for any roof over their head, more intent on getting back downstairs to check on Josh than where she might actually sleep that night.

Now the desire to curl up in the nest of pillows and

blanket Maggie had arranged next to the bed, to pull the blanket over her head and try to get some sleep, was tempting. Who knew when they would have a safe roof over their head again? But there was too much whirling in her mind for her to think she would get any sleep, and there was too much to do, anyway. Josh would be ready to travel again in the morning, he insisted, and while Elizabeth wanted to make him stay put longer, until Kit gave him a clean bill of health, she knew that he was right. Not only did they have to be moving for Maggie's sake, and his own, but for their hosts' safety, as well.

Ray would kill anyone who stood between him and Maggie. Elizabeth understood that now, finally. Just the memory of those beasts made her shudder. Whatever Ray was doing, or planning, whatever his sidelong looks and veiled comments about her sister meant, it was worse than no good.

The only way to make sure that Maggie was safe was to make her disappear.

And Josh… She had to make sure that he got back on the search. The idea tore something inside her, hot and painful. She had only just met the man. Unicorn. Mustang. He wasn't even human…. But he was true, and kind, and loyal, and loving. And he loved her. Or he thought he did.

There was a padded bench under the window, and she settled herself on that, looking out into the night. The bare lines of fields and distant trees, black ink on paler black paper, was soothing. She rested her forehead against the cool glass, and tried to sort out her own emotions.

Did she love Josh? Was this agony inside her, this physical need, love? What about the sense of calmness, of being safe and protected, that she felt when he was nearby? She didn't know. For the first time she wished she had read romance novels as a teenager instead of history books, or listened when the other girls gossiped in the bathroom. Her experiences with love had been gentler, sweeter than this—but they had been with gentler, sweeter boys. Josh—Mustang—was neither sweet, nor a boy.

And he wanted her.

And he needed to take a virgin mate.

Could she live with that? Could she be in love with someone who couldn't be with her—or had to be shared?

No. Elizabeth knew herself well enough to know the answer to that, even without the pain in her midsection when she asked the question. She did not share well. But if she held on to him…he would lose his humanity. And while she understood that the Mustang was as much a part of him as…as her dreaming, or Maggie's ability to reach animals, that wasn't the form she wanted to spend the rest of her life with.

And she did want to spend the rest of her life with him, Elizabeth discovered. She wanted to wake in the morning and see him watching her, to be able to reach out during the day and touch his hand, hear his voice, listen to his words and have him hear hers. To tumble into bed at night and feel his skin against hers, the soft sound of his breathing, even to be annoyed when he tried to take up more of the bed, or left the toilet seat up, or...

Was that love? She thought that maybe it was, and it terrified her, the depth of it, sudden and unanticipated.

"Mother, what should I do?"

The image of her mother—tall and lean, her dark hair prematurely graying but her face barely lined— came to her. The way her mother had looked before the illness, before everything went bad. The last time they had sat down over cookies and tea and talked, girl talk, her father banished to the TV room with Maggie and a bowl of popcorn, the two of them giggling like kids....

"What should I do?"

Follow your dreams, her mother's memory told her. *Your dreams have always been true.*

Her mother had never known of her eldest daughter's dreaming, had never given that particular encouragement. The memory wasn't real. And she had only dreamed of bad things, since the flu struck. Worrisome things, terrifying things.

Except when the Mustang stood guard over them. The thought came to her, and despite herself her lips curled up in a smile. When Josh was nearby, her dreams were peaceful and sweet.

Her dreams told her what to do.

Her head resting against the windowpane, Elizabeth closed her eyes, and slipped into a light doze.

Josh woke, aware that something was wrong. He lay still, trying to hear what had woken him. His body felt fine—sore and achy, but no pain anywhere. The room was still and quiet, and from the echoes of that silence he guessed that the entire house was asleep, and it was somewhere past midnight. The rut stirred with him, making his body cramp a little, but he was used to that now, and shoved it aside to follow whatever had woken him.

Was it as simple as being in a strange bed? Did he have to use the bathroom, or was he hungry? Josh ran through the checklist in a matter of seconds, and dismissed those options. No. Something else had woken him.

Josh...

There. Just a whisper of a scent, more than a memory but less than a voice... Elizabeth.

She was dreaming of him. He knew it the way he knew which way the wind was blowing, or where fresh water could be found. She had called his name in her dream, and he had responded.

The rut flared again, as though angry at him, and he doubled over from the pain of it, this time. It would not be denied much longer; the urge to shift into Mustang form was stronger, almost out of his control.

"Not yet," he told it. "I need to get them somewhere safe."

His earlier decision had been the best option, even if Elizabeth didn't agree. He would convince her to join the herd. Grace would take them in. She would know what to do. And the herd could protect them against any monster their enemy might send against them.

Josh thought of Maggie playing with the yearlings, of Elizabeth walking with his sisters, and he smiled despite the pain.

Josh!

That was no peaceful whisper, and he sat upright in bed, ignoring the pain that shot upward from his ribs at the sudden movement. Elizabeth needed him.

One minute she had been drifting, a soft, peaceful doze where she walked on soft grass, the sun bright and warm overhead, the air clean and smelling of fresh straw and wet dirt, a warm body moving next to her, making her feel safe and protected, and the next she was surrounded by howling monsters in a dark space, alone and bereft of any hope at all. A huge, clawed hand came out of the darkness to swipe at her, and she was suddenly aware that she was supposed to be taking care of Maggie, she had promised her parents she would take care of Maggie, where was Maggie?

"Josh!"

Even as she called for help, Elizabeth was waking up, aware that she was in the spare bedroom in the farmhouse, that there were no monsters, that Maggie was in the bed asleep....

Elizabeth turned slowly, and looked at the bed, and the lump half-hidden under the covers.

Maggie was a sprawler. She used every inch of every bed she slept in. She never stayed so still for that long....

Elizabeth was across the room, pulling back the covers, already knowing what she would find before the body-shaped pillows were revealed, a white sheet of paper resting on top of one.

She turned again, knowing that Josh was in the doorway, barely even realizing that he was stark naked in his rush to respond.

"She's gone!"

The note had been blunt and to the point: *It's because of me. I can tell where the bad animals are, and I think they can find me, too. They only want me. You'll be safe now, and you can get Josh home in time, so he's okay, too. It's what Grandpa would have done. I love you. Maggie.*

"Your grandfather was a brave man, I take it?"

Elizabeth was furious and terrified, all at once. "He decided he didn't like the world he lived in, so he did something to change it. But he was never stupid about it, and he didn't try to get himself killed. What was she thinking?" Her voice was barely a whisper; they didn't want to risk waking their hosts, and having to explain this new development.

Josh touched her elbow, lightly, a feather touch, but it calmed her immediately. "They'll find her. She's right about that. That's the only way they could have caught up with us so easily—if those creatures could sense her, too. But they won't hurt her, Elizabeth. Not if this Ray is controlling them."

"You fought them," she said. "Do you really think anything can control them? His men shot one, rather than risk it coming back at them. They…"

"He won't let anything happen to her. Especially if she doesn't resist. They'll bring her back to him without harm, and he will keep her safe." A prisoner, but safe.

"Then I have to go back and get her out again," Elizabeth said grimly. "And this time I don't care who knows about it, about whatever it is he's doing. I'll tear the Community apart if I have to, in order to make sure she's safe." She didn't care what it took, who she had to hurt, so long as her sister was free. The fierceness of it shook her to her core, and she welcomed it.

"We'll go get her."

That put a halt on Elizabeth's bloody-minded thoughts, and she shook her head in refusal. "You can't. You have to…"

"Elizabeth." He reached for her, pulling her unresisting body into his arms, and she was suddenly very aware that he was clad only in a sheet he had pulled off the bed and wrapped around his waist, and that underneath that sheet, his erection was stirring. "Elizabeth, don't fight me on this. Maggie's safety is the most important thing. And whatever or wherever these beasts come from, it has to be dealt with, before anyone else gets hurt. Everything else…nothing else matters. Not right now. You know that. We both do."

She rested her cheek against his chest, feeling the warm skin, and the steady pulse of his heart. There was no sense of peace in this embrace, but she felt her determination, her strength, returning, nonetheless.

"We'll go get her back," she said, agreeing. "And shut Ray down, once and for all."

Even if her dreams said otherwise.

Chapter 13

It had been four days since they left the Community. Elizabeth felt, somewhat unfairly, that it should take them four days to get back. Instead, rolling down the highway in Kit's old pickup truck, they were there within a few hours. So much time, and they had only managed to get that far? If she had pushed harder, if she had used their money to buy bus tickets somewhere far away, if she hadn't relied on local contacts that betrayed them anyway…would Maggie be safe? Would they have escaped Ray's reach? Would…

"You can second-guess yourself until the sun burns out," Josh said, somehow knowing exactly what she was thinking, reaching out with the hand not on the steering wheel and lifting her hand to his mouth, kissing her knuckles gently. "It doesn't help. You did the best you could, and Maggie should have known better than to pull such a boneheaded stunt." He let go of her hand and added, grimly, "Once she's safe, I'm going to put her over my knee."

"I'd pay money to see that," she said, but despite his reassurances, and the tingling sensation in her fingertips, her heart still ached with self-blame. "And I feel bad about the truck," she murmured, looking out the window as the sun rose over the trees to their right, the sky turning to a clear blue as night was chased away. As long as she was wallowing, might as well do it properly.

"You would have felt worse if we'd stopped to wake them up and try to explain what was going on," Josh said. He was right, but it didn't make her feel any less like a bad houseguest. The note they had left had been unavoidably brief, and it wasn't as though either of them had enough cash to leave that would make a difference, assuming the older couple was even willing to take it.

"We'll get Maggie back, we'll return the truck, and you and Maggie will be free of this bastard forever," Josh said, but despite the hard confidence in his voice, she couldn't take any comfort from his words. The surety of her dreams was fading with every mile they came closer to Ray, as though his very presence was enough to suck the strength out of her. Needing something to do, she rummaged through the glove compartment, finding the insurance and registration information, and a small notebook and pen. Tearing out a sheet of paper, she printed *Please return to owners, with our apologies* on it, then wrapped the paper around the documents and put it back in the glove compartment. If the cops found the truck, if, for whatever reason she couldn't return the vehicle in person…

Not thoughts she wanted to have, but Elizabeth had never shied away from unpleasant truth before, and she wasn't going to now. Ray would kill Josh without blinking. He would kill her, too, if he felt he didn't need her anymore. He wouldn't kill Maggie, not so long as he needed her…but what kind of life would she have? What…

"We'll find her, we'll get her out of there." Josh didn't look away from the road, but his right hand left the wheel again, touching the back of her hand.

Elizabeth closed her eyes. "He has more of those monsters."

"You don't know that."

"Yes. I do." She did. Somehow, she knew. And she knew that he wasn't going to pull them back this time. Whatever he had been planning, it wasn't going to stay hidden much longer.

His hand covered hers more securely, although he never took his eyes off the road, and she leaned back against the seat and tried not to think too much.

They skirted the nearest town, and pulled over about halfway between there and the borders of Community land. The two-lane road was bordered by woods on one side, and farmland on the other, and had a wide shoulder for emergency stops.

"We can walk from here," Josh said, taking the keys out of the ignition and placing them on the console between the two seats.

By the time Elizabeth got out of the truck, Josh had already gone to the back, and pulled out a small metal box.

"What's that?" she asked, even as he used a rock to break open the lock. He opened the lid, and her question was answered: inside the box was a small handgun... black metal, deadly-looking. He ignored her indrawn gasp of shock, and lifted the gun out, then swiftly, with the ease of a man who knew what he was doing, removed a box of ammunition from the case and loaded the bullets in a precise manner.

"Here." He handed it to her, and she took it, almost automatically. It didn't weigh as much as she thought it would, and her hand closed around the grip without conscious thought.

"You ever shoot anything before?"

"A rifle," she said. "When I was younger. We all learned, a safety class in school. But not since then, and never..."

Never to point at a person. Never to point at any living thing, just a paper target.

"It's the same theory," he said. "Point firmly, pull gently."

She didn't want to take the gun, wanted to drop it, throw it away, scream at him for giving it to her.

For Maggie, she took it.

The safety was on, so she felt somewhat comfortable fitting it into the side pocket of her backpack, wrapped in an extra T-shirt to make sure nothing could jostle it. Not easy to reach in case of an emergency, but if it were that much of an emergency she wasn't sure what use the gun would be, anyway.

The monsters had claws and teeth that could take down a unicorn. What could she, a thin-skinned, defenseless human, do against them?

Elizabeth shook herself, mentally. She had a brain. She could think, and plan. Those monsters, they didn't seem smart, just animal cunning. They relied on someone else giving them orders. How? How was Ray controlling them?

When she looked up again, Josh had stepped back, and had the look in his eye she was already able to recognize: he was about to shift. Apparently "walking from here" meant that he would walk, and she would ride.

She forced herself to watch the transformation carefully, trying to see a moment when Josh went to Mustang, some instant when the human became unicorn. But no matter how she tried not to blink, it all blurred, the magic that allowed the transformation shimmering and blurring her view, so that it seemed like an almost seamless transition, one to the other.

Impossible, that the bulk and mass of the unicorn

could be contained within Josh's strong but human form. She had touched that body, felt it, cared for it... and she had ridden the Mustang. They were nothing alike. And yet, they were the same.

He snorted at her, clearly saying *stop gawking and mount up.* So she did, tangling her fingers in his mane and using the bumper of the truck as a mounting block. His back was warm, the feel of his neck under her hands familiar, and when he started walking, Elizabeth realized that her body moved with his almost naturally, as though she had been on horseback—unicorn-back— her entire life.

She leaned forward to whisper in one pointed ear. "Your four-legged form is useful. But I'm not going to let you be stuck in it for the rest of your life."

The ear twitched once, backward, then returned to a determined forward angle, and she got a very clear sense of him telling her to stop worrying about him and focus on what they were going to do. She rested her cheek against his muscled neck, and let him carry her the remaining miles, trying to focus only on Maggie. For Maggie, there would be no fear.

"Scout reports incursion at the western boundary."

"Thank you."

The Community scorned excessive technology. Mostly Ray approved of that—he might want to change the way some things were done, but he had no beef with the original aims of the Community, to rely on self, rather than external devices. He did admit, though, that being able to set up electronic sensors around his property would make guarding it much easier.

However, the beasts did the job almost as well; while they could not give him specifics, they could sniff out anything new or unusual well before it reached the main buildings, and their noses were never wrong.

Maggie was seated on the couch across the room from him, her left arm bound in a silver manacle, the chain leashing her to the heavy piece of furniture. She had walked in of her own accord, but he did not trust her to stay there. She looked at him with those dark eyes, and the venom in them made him smile.

"You don't even know how miraculous you are," he said softly. "All my work, all my effort to create the perfect merger of man and beast, is nothing compared to you, and you merely…appeared."

"I'm normal," she said, her voice as cold as anything her sister could have managed at her most spitting mad. "Your monsters are—"

"Monsters. I know." He nodded in agreement, refusing to take offense. "They are the best I could do, with what I had available. But with you here to control them, we will be able to breed them better. We'll raise them to the next level, and learn how to help humanity at the same time. Isn't that what the Community was founded to do? To make humanity better?"

Maggie closed her eyes and rested her head against the back of the couch. "Whatever."

She had no intention of helping him. He knew that. But he also knew how to convince her otherwise.

"Your sister is on her way to rescue you."

He was gratified to see her eyes open again at that. He didn't know for certain that it was Elizabeth who had been scented, but really, who else could it be? He had known them since they were children, and the one thing he knew for certain about Elizabeth was that she would die rather than abandon her sister.

"You're lying."

"Maggie. I'm hurt. I have never lied to you." He hadn't. He had never lied to anyone. Mainly because nobody had ever asked him the questions they didn't want answered. They took his leadership and the benefits that came with it, and never wondered out loud what means had gotten them there. Perfect sheep, all of them. But sheep were boring, after a while. At least Elizabeth and Maggie gave him a challenge. Maybe he should consider breeding them as well as his monsters.

The thought made him smile. Maggie was too young, and too useful in other areas, but Elizabeth, now there was an idea. He might even breed her himself, once Maggie was secured. If she wouldn't leave her sister, she definitely would never leave her children. A bonus: that bond would tie the still-undecided members of the Community even more to him; he had no personal desire for a wife or children, but to become part of the Sweet dynasty, father of the fifth generation of the Founder's

Line? Yes. A pity he hadn't thought to do that before the girls ran....

"You should be scared, if they're coming," she said then, and closed her eyes again, but he could see the strain in her body, dispelling any illusion that she wasn't worried. Ray watched her a moment longer, then turned back to the man who had brought him the news, who had been standing there quietly since then. Glen would never think to oppose Ray, or object to any decision his leader made, but Ray could see that holding a teenaged girl in shackles did not please his assistant. Especially since he had known that girl since she was a newborn.

"Have the sentinels back off," Ray told him. "If it is Elizabeth, she is not to be harmed."

He had always known that he could not have Maggie without Elizabeth. Her parents might eventually have been swayed by his promises, his appeal to their parents' original goals for the Community, to raise generations that were stronger, smarter, wiser than their parents, and his contention that Maggie was the unexpected, almost despaired-of step toward their future.

But Elizabeth would never see Maggie as anything other than her baby sister, and would never have let him guide the girl's future without her input. So be it. He was a reasonable man, but there were only so many allowances and compromises he could make. Now it was time to show his hand.

They had just left the cover of the tree line, and stepped into the backyard of the Yancy house, a small white clapboard house with a huge garden Elizabeth remembered weeding when she was a kid, to earn a few dollars, when Mustang stopped. Elizabeth slid down off his back even as the shift took place, and Josh was standing next to her.

"Leave your bag here," he told her. "We'll come back for it later."

She nodded, not trusting her voice. Placing the bag on the ground at the edge of the garden, where it would be hidden by the tangle of tomato plants, she reached in and retrieved the pistol. It felt heavier now, in her hand, and the cool metal made her shudder.

For Maggie, she thought. To save Maggie. She slid it into the front pocket of her sweatshirt.

"Come on," Josh said. "You know the town. Where would they keep her?"

Elizabeth had to stop and think. "Nowhere public," she said, and her voice cracked embarrassingly on the last word. "If anyone saw her they'd ask where I was. And Maggie…she's not going to keep quiet, not even if threatened. She's got a mouth on her."

"I'd noticed that," Josh said, and squeezed her hand gently, to show that he was joking.

"So he'd want her secured, but private. Not his own house—he has a housekeeper I can't think would put up with that, Mrs. Malloy's ancient but fierce and knows Maggie too well. Everyone knows everyone else…. He'd need somewhere that was private but secure, but he could still be without anyone asking questions…he's not going to let her out of his sight if he can help it."

She hadn't known that she knew Ray's thought process so well, but the moment the question was asked the answers came to her, the same way her dreams did, without hesitation or doubt.

"So…his office? You said he was the local herd stallion, is there a place that people only go by his invitation?"

"No. That's the point of the Community, everything's open to every other member. Anyone can walk into the committee offices, and… No. Wait."

She stopped, and stared up at the sky, thinking. "I remember my father talking once, about a meeting he'd been to. Before the flu came and he got sick. He made a joke about going underground, that they were meeting underground because Ray hated sunlight so much—he's pale, and burns easily," she explained to Josh. "But I don't know of any place that's underground—most of the houses here don't even have cellars because it's all rock underneath. The only place it could have been was the hall—there's a storm cellar there, but it's never been used, not in all the time I can remember."

"And nobody would think twice about this bastard spending time in the hall?"

"His office is on the second floor," she said. "If he's not home, he's usually there."

He started to walk forward, but she grabbed at his elbow, pulling him back. "Not that way. Here." There was a dirt path that led around the town, that all the kids used when they were ditching class, or just wanted to stay out of sight of the adults. It had been years since Elizabeth had used it herself, but it was still there. They had to duck under low-hanging branches, and squeeze through some narrow passages behind garages and tool sheds, but eventually it wound them around town, to within sight of the two-story Community Hall, and Ray's office.

"There."

There were a scattering of people on the street, as was normal on a weekday morning, people running errands or on their way to and from work. School had just started, and a few tardy teenagers went by on their bikes…it was all peaceful, almost serene. Exactly the way she remembered it all the years of her childhood. Her bakery was there, the quiet little storefront with the dark blue awning, and she was pleased to see activity inside.

Josh sniffed at the air, as though he'd be able to pick out Maggie's scent, and then blushed a little when he realized what he was doing. "I'd feel better if I could shift," he said. "I'd be more useful to you."

"You're here. I'm not doing this alone." The idea of facing Ray by herself made Elizabeth quail. Having Josh beside her… "No matter what form you're in," she said, "you're Mustang. Herd stallion, protector of yearlings and smasher of monsters."

The words had come without conscious thought, trying to distract herself from what they were about to do, so she was completely unprepared for Josh's reaction. Before she had finished speaking, he had her pushed up against the wall of the house they were standing by, out of sight of casual bystanders, his hands holding her wrists up against the wall, his lower body pressing her flat, keeping her from resisting. Not that she had intended to, even if she wasn't so astonished.

"Wha—?" she started to ask, and then his mouth descended on hers. Not gently, not sweetly, but with a fierce rush that took the rest of her breath away. Had anyone else done that, laid hands and mouth on her like that, she would have resisted, fought back, possibly with a knee to their delicate area. But the anger and frustration she could feel in him, in that kiss, was tempered by something even more primal, more ferocious, and it melted her resistance and roused an equally fierce response within her.

She might not be able to move her hands, but she was able to hook one leg around his, bringing his body in closer, feeling the heat coming off his skin and the friction of his body stroking against hers. Never mind that anyone could see them, anyone could find them, utterly defenseless. Right now, all she wanted was the press of his body against hers, the roughness of his mouth bruising hers, and to be able to give back as good as she got, letting him know that she felt the same, the hunger and the urgency and the hot flame of desire—and something more, something she had no words for, no way to understand, but accepted as part of what was between them, a blade-sharp slice into her soul that stung and yet felt good all at once, a sensual pain that made no sense but could only be indulged in.

Her words had triggered it, somehow, but the kiss made it real.

Was this the rut he had talked about? If so, she didn't know how he could stand it, how he could resist it. All she wanted was to shed their clothes, to have him inside her, to surround him entirely, to take him inside until he could never leave…and know that she would never be washed from his skin, either, that he would never look at another woman without remembering the feel of her, the touch, the *need*….

"Stop, stop…" he muttered, but she couldn't tell if he was talking to her, or himself. "Not now. God, ah…" He dove in for another lingering kiss, this one ending more gently, his mouth moving down the line of her throat, his tongue picking up the drops of sweat as though they were precious liquor. Then he found the strength to step back, his hands dropping away from her arms, his entire body shuddering like he had just run a marathon.

Her body felt the same way, and she didn't know if she could walk, or if her bones would melt from the heat.

"Maggie first," he said, drawing a deep breath. His eyes looked almost black with emotion, and his face was drawn into determined lines. "Maggie, and then... we are going to deal with this, Elizabeth."

With that oath, he took her hand, and they stepped back out into the street.

They hadn't made it more than halfway across when a man started walking behind them, his pace steady, not quite threatening but obviously following them. Another woman came from the left, pacing them, as well.

"Steady," Josh murmured into Elizabeth's ear. "They're just humans. You've already beaten them before, and they know it. They're going to be cautious of you, because you kicked their asses."

It wasn't even close to true, but the warm feel of his breath did more than the actual sound of his words or the knowledge of the gun still in her pocket, and Elizabeth kept her own step strong and calm, her back straight and her head high, as though she was walking down the street on her way to the bakery, her day spread out ahead of her with peace and contentment. Nobody needed to know that she was terrified inside.

She would never give Ray or his crew the satisfaction—or risk being rejected, the others still unable to see the horror underneath that smooth voice and smile.

They entered the Hall, and she heard several people call out her name, but didn't stop, merely raised one hand in greeting and moved on. Her feet took her, unerringly, not toward Ray's office, but toward a door in the back of the main hallway, one she had never been in before. Josh walked with her, his body shielding her from any attacks their unwanted companions might make, but the two guards merely walked alongside, falling back when they reached the door, as though they had not been given permission to go any farther.

The door opened under her hand without resistance, leading into a short, well-lit hallway, and a flight of stairs leading down.

"Step into my parlor, said the spider to the fly...." Elizabeth said softly.

"I swat spiders with my tail," Josh said flatly in response.

Together, they stepped into the hallway, and went down the stairs.

The space below the Hall might once have been a storm shelter, but someone had spent a lot of money upgrading it recently, probably when Ray brought in all the medical supplies to battle the flu epidemic. The walls were finished and painted, the lights updated to indirect fluorescents like an office building and the floor a smooth white linoleum that echoed their footsteps against the walls. The space had been broken up into several frosted-glass cubicles, and over the tops Elizabeth could see desktops with laptop computers and printers, and ergonomic chairs set as though the occupants had just gone out to grab lunch. It looked so...ordinary.

Then a muffled roar broke the silence, and they both

stopped. Elizabeth fought down the urge to flee back up the stairs and slam the door behind her.

"If you bolt, I will, too," Josh said.

"Are you kidding me?"

"Lead mare leads the way. I'm just here to hit things."

"Making me laugh is not helpful," she said sternly, but found that her own shaking had disappeared.

The next roar sounded different, higher-pitched and angrier, and she could pinpoint it this time, as coming from the far wall, where there was a row of seven white doors, each with a large window at the top, and an electronic keypad set where the handle should have been.

"They're down here. Oh, God…"

Josh made a move as though to go investigate, and she grabbed at his arm to hold him back. If they were behind doors, hopefully those doors were locked. Why tempt fate?

Then the sound of another door opening off to their left made them both stop.

"Libby. It's been too long. I'm so glad you came home."

She turned to face the speaker, feeling Josh move with her. "Ray." Her voice didn't shake or show any tremor at all; they might have been meeting in the grocery store, for all the emotion she let escape.

He stood there, tall and elegant, and as honest-looking as ever in his khakis and dress shirt. Even knowing everything she knew, having seen the things she had seen, it was difficult not to trust him. "Who is your friend?" he said. "I don't think we've met?"

"Where's Maggie?" she asked, not answering him or bothering with introductions.

"In my office, waiting for you. Please, come in, both of you."

The last thing that Elizabeth wanted to do was follow him anywhere. But he was beckoning them inside the door he had come through, and if Maggie was there, they had no choice but to follow.

She was uncomfortably aware of the gun still in her sweatshirt pouch, and how long it would take her to reach in and take it out, much less aim and shoot.

Behind the door was a large office, as sumptuous as the rest of the space was barren, and Maggie, sitting on a small sofa. She looked unharmed, and Elizabeth ran to her, only to discover, when she tried to hug her sister, that the younger girl was chained to the seat.

"Damn you, unlock her!"

"I'm afraid I can't do that, not yet, anyway. It does pain me to offer her such hospitality, but I'm not quite convinced that she means to stay, and I really must insist that she remain. It's not safe for her, wandering around the outside world like that. Really, Libby, what were you thinking, taking her out there?"

"I'm sorry, Libby," her sister said mournfully. "I heard what Josh said, about…" Her voice trailed off, not wanting to spill any secrets, and a tear dripped from the corner of her eye. "Why didn't you run?"

Elizabeth turned her back on Ray, trusting Josh to keep an eye on the other man, and gathered Maggie into her arms again. "Idiot. Did you really think I'd leave you alone? Did you think either of us was just going to abandon you?"

There was a sniffle from somewhere against her shoulder, then Maggie pulled away, trying to wipe at her eyes with her unbound hand. "I was dumb, huh?"

"Very."

And now they were back in Ray's hands, surrounded by his people; exactly where they hadn't wanted to be. Maggie looked like she was going to burst into full-blown tears now that she no longer had to be tough and defiant, and Elizabeth touched the edge of her nose with one finger, forcing a smile. "Eight legs are better than six," she said, and hoped that Maggie understood.

Josh heard Elizabeth, too, but he wasn't sure if he would be able to follow through. There wasn't enough room in the office to shift, not with all four of them, and the furniture, and he didn't want to risk hitting Maggie or Elizabeth with his hooves accidentally.

Ray, he'd have no trouble hitting. In fact, the Mustang very much wanted to plant a hoof right in the middle of his well-bred, superficially pleasant face. He understood now what Elizabeth had meant, when she said that he was too well liked. Whatever this man was really thinking or planning, he never let it reach the surface. He was like a prairie dog; seemingly harmless, but constantly digging holes underfoot, until the entire ground was riddled, and you had no safe footing when you ran.

"We haven't been introduced. My name is Ray Barist." He held out one well-manicured hand, and Josh took it, but didn't offer his name in return.

"Ah. The strong, silent type?" Ray chuckled, as though he had said something amusing, then let go of Josh's hand and turned back to Elizabeth. "A pity you didn't bring your little war-pony, too. I was quite curious to see if my people were hallucinating, or if you had actually managed to capture a unicorn.... That must have been Maggie's doing, of course. We all know that you're not exactly unicorn bait, are you, Libby, dear?"

He said it in the same pleasant tone of voice as previous that it took Josh a moment to realize what the bastard had just said. Fury surged in his veins, and the shift threatened to take over without his consent, but the small smile on Elizabeth's face calmed him. She wasn't upset at the insult. In fact, she looked almost...amused.

"Is that the best you can do, Ray? Really?"

She looked calm and in control, but he could see the way the hand on Maggie's arm trembled, just slightly, and he could smell the fear on her skin, rising in the air. The instinct to charge to her aid, to snort and paw at the ground and warn this snake off, threatened to overload his brain. No. He was in control, not his instincts. He needed to stay in human form, to stay human....

"You're supposed to be so brilliant, such a great

leader, and all you can do is sew together a few piti-ful creatures, and insult the fact that I'm a healthy woman with a sex life? That's your idea of being a supervillain?"

"A supervillain? Is that what you think I am?" The snake sounded surprised, and almost hurt. "All I am trying to do is continue the work your very own grand-father began. Work, I might add, that your own parents were part of—but sadly has fallen by the wayside." He took the pose of a professor, patient and wise. "Your grandfather had a vision—that was what the Commu-nity was for, to be a laboratory, an incubator for his dreams. To create a society where the very best poten-tial is encouraged, where humans can develop into the utmost of our abilities."

He smiled at Maggie, and Josh felt his skin crawl at the look in the man's eyes. It wasn't sexual—Elizabeth had been right about that. It was worse.

"Little Maggie here." His gaze intensified, and the girl shuddered under the weight of it. "So very special. Do you even know how special she is? All the work I have done on my creatures over the years—the ones you dismiss as 'pitiful'—and she comes along quite natu-rally, the perfect combination of genetics, and shows me the next step to take. She will help me to create a generation that is able to accomplish anything, mind and body. Maggie will do great things here, my dear, I assure you."

"Over my dead body," Elizabeth said, still calm, her

gaze steady on Ray, watching him the way a cat would watch a fox too near her kittens.

"Libby, Libby. Again, you overreact. Why do you insist on thinking that I want to harm her?" He leaned forward, his hands flat on his desk. "No, no, I will take care of Maggie as though she were my very own. She will lack for nothing."

"So long as she does what you say."

"That is how it works, yes." Ray didn't seem to see anything wrong with that statement. "I am the alpha male. It is your responsibility to follow me. I am the Community's chosen leader."

There was a distinctly feminine snort at that, but Josh couldn't tell if it was from Maggie or Elizabeth, as he had been distracted by a sound behind him. Human hearing wouldn't have picked it up, but it was like gunshot to his sensitive hearing: the sound of electronic dead bolts being released, one after another.

The need to shift was screaming at him, but there was no room, and no way to predict how Ray would react. Did he have a gun? A knife? More henchmen like the ones who had shadowed them into the building waiting for his call?

Or was he relying on the creatures Josh could smell creeping toward the office door, even now?

Elizabeth could protect herself, could run, but Maggie was still chained to that damned sofa. They had to get her free, somehow.

"Where did they come from, Barist?" He only wanted

to get the man's attention off his females, to see his face, read his intentions there, but the question, once asked, was vitally important. "Your beasties. What did you use to create them?"

"Oh, a bit here and a bit there," he said casually, turning to look at Josh, but not moving away from the girls. "The topic always fascinated me, even as a child, and when I came here, reading on the history of the Founding, it all came into focus."

He looked so calm, so normal, it was impossible to comprehend what he was really saying.

"My own training was limited, but once I became chair of the hospital committee, I was fortunate enough to have access to very talented medical technicians, who found the chance to experiment with human tissue…irresistible."

"Whose tissue?" Elizabeth asked, her voice low and horrified. "You bastard, whose tissue did you use?"

"Every member of the Community volunteered," Ray said, refusing to become defensive. "By coming here, by being a part, you also agreed to be part of the ongoing experiment. I merely accelerated the pace."

Elizabeth took the attack again. "You used our friends, neighbors… Oh, God. Were they still alive when you did that to them? Was the flu your fault? Did you make them sick so they'd go into your hospital, be under your care?" Her voice shook, a mixture of outrage and disgust. "How many people died because of what you did?"

"Elizabeth. Stop your hysterics. I did not cause the flu. It was a tragic outbreak, likely brought home from school by one of the children. Closed communities are prone to those sorts of thing, and you know I warned the committee about it, time and again. I urged everyone to get flu shots—including your parents.

"Every person in my study was a volunteer. Some gave less, some more. But they all believed in what we are doing."

Josh saw, out of the corner of his eye, Maggie trying to work her slender wrist free of the manacle. Her skin was red and bruised-looking, indicating that she had tried before, and not been successful.

"And do they still? Do they still believe, once you'd twisted them, and then locked them in cages—and set them on their neighbors, to kill?" Elizabeth stepped directly in front of Maggie, blocking her from view.

"If you hadn't run, there would have been no need to send them after you. You've only yourself to blame for any damage done."

"And what's Maggie's role in this? Why do you want her, really? It's not to talk to those things of yours, is it?"

Josh could hear the footfalls outside, the soft wet sniffing of a predator scenting the air. The need to shift was making him tense and edgy, but he had to maintain control. If this bastard knew what he was, there would be no escape for any of them. There was a small grunt of pain, and then the snick of metal against wood. Was Maggie free?

"She is the natural next step in the Community's genetic experiment. Her skills tie into our animal nature, control it. Her beast is inside, while mine are external. What rests within her genes, when matched with my discoveries, will create the perfect blend of man and animal, beast and intellect, able to call on the best elements of each."

Josh went cold. This bastard wasn't trying to create a superhuman. He was trying to create a were. Like him. Like the herd. Not consciously, not the actual shift, maybe, but far too close for comfort.

He looked up and met Elizabeth's horrified gaze. She had the same thought, he knew it as though she had screamed it out loud. It wasn't just about getting Maggie out of there, not anymore. If he discovered what Josh was, if he learned about the herd…

If he would do this to his own neighbors, and call it good, what would he do to strangers? To beings who had already achieved his goal?

Josh had heard more than enough. Nobody else would suffer because of this bastard and his sick experiments. This ended, here and now.

"Barist," Josh said softly. When the man turned to face him, he shifted.

Chapter 14

Elizabeth knew what Josh was going to do even before she saw his form shimmer. Daring to turn her back on Ray, hoping he would be distracted, she knelt by Maggie's side. Her sister was holding her arm cradled to her chest, tearstains on her face and an expression of weary pain marking her features.

The manacle dangled off the arm of the sofa, its cuff empty, but still locked.

"I think I broke something," Maggie said softly, and swallowed hard, like she was about to throw up. Her eyes were glazed over, not focusing properly.

"Can you stand up?"

"Dunno. Maybe."

There was a crash behind them, the sound of a door

bursting open and a loud, animal scream followed by a shrill challenge that could only have come from Mustang's throat. Maggie focused briefly, and gasped, shrinking back against the sofa back. Elizabeth turned on her heels, and scrambled back next to her, instinctively. Josh had shifted, his thickly muscled body turned sideways and standing between them and the door, his maned neck arched, head down, his horn held at a steady angle; warning enemies away. There were three monsters in the room with them, crowding the space even more. One was even more catlike than the earlier beast, its body crouched, a long tail flickering behind it, the ears set on a human skull tufted and twitching. The human mouth was filled with sharp teeth, the kind that were meant only for taking down prey, and rending flesh.

The other two monsters were more humanlike, but only by comparison. They hung back by the door, unable to get past the cat-monster, but preventing anyone from making a break. There was the only one exit, and that led back into the lab, where who knew how many other of the monsters waited.

They were trapped.

Ray had moved back behind his desk, and he held a large, odd-shaped gun, the long muzzle pointed down at the ground, but Elizabeth had no doubt that it could and would rise up in an instant. A tranquilizer gun, to control the beasts? If so, the level of drugs in it would likely kill a human easily. Or a Mustang.

Her gun…could she get at it? If she even reached for it, would Ray shoot her? The weight seemed to burn in her pocket, but she dared not move.

"Bad animals," Maggie said, her voice a whimper. "Bad animals. I can't control them. I can't…" Her voice broke, the combination of fear and pain overloading her.

"Maggie, listen to me." Elizabeth spoke quickly, not taking her eyes off the tableau before them. Any instant, one of them would move, and then all hell would break loose. "I need you to do something and I need you to do it without hesitation. You have to get out of here. You're small and fast, get past them when the fighting starts, and then run like hell. Don't stop, don't come back."

"But…"

"Maggie, listen to me. Don't stop. Don't ask anyone here for help. Get out of town and go straight to the cops. Tell them… Tell them you were abused, you're afraid of Ray."

It was true, although not in any way the outside world would understand. Maggie was just a kid; they would protect her, even if they didn't believe it, and Ray had no legal right to custody. She'd be safe. And maybe, maybe, someone else would listen, would stop Ray, if they failed.

Maggie, bless her, didn't protest, but slid off the sofa, crouching, looking for her opening.

The cat-creature leaped, and Mustang's horn lowered, and the room exploded into chaos.

Vaguely, Elizabeth was aware of Maggie scrambling

for the door, her injured arm tucked like a broken wing, but she had no time to do more than send her love with the younger girl, because the cat-creature had leaped not at Mustang, but at her. The oversized hands, with their curved claws, were stretched out toward her face, coming down like the Reaper's scythe, and she felt the whisper of them across her cheek, the salty tang of blood under her nose, before she was falling, and Mustang's body was over hers, his hooves slamming the cat-monster against the wall. Screams filled the room, echoing off the walls, until her ears rung with the noise and she couldn't think straight. But when she blinked again, she saw great heavy furred feet coming toward her, and she reacted, lunging from her prone position to grab one of those legs with both hands, her fingers grabbing at the thick hair and yanking with all her strength.

"Gahhh, bitch," she thought she heard the monster say, as it leaned down to try to dislodge her. Its mouth had trouble forming words, but it clearly understood English, and something inside her died a little. This might have been a friend, once, a teacher, a customer at the bakery....

She forced that thought to die, and sank her teeth into the furred leg.

The creature howled, and swatted at her head, making her ears ring again, but she refused to let go, gagging a little at the taste, like sweaty laundry and salt water, and slightly rancid meat. It staggered, and she released her bite, and then used her upper body to shove at it, where she thought its knees might be. They fell over in a tangle, and Elizabeth felt its hands grabbing at her body—thankfully without claws; this was one of the other creatures, not the cat-thing—trying to crush her bones. She squirmed, trying to eel away, trying to get the gun out of the pocket, but her hands were so numb with fear, she could barely get a grip on it. The blood from her scratches dripped into her eyes, and she blinked, unable to see.

There was a crash somewhere off to her left, and a man's yell, making her hand jerk, the gun going flying across the floor.

"Damn it!"

She scrambled on the floor, trying to find the gun, anything to use as a weapon. A piece of something— wood, splintered, the leg of a broken chair—met her searching fingers, and she grabbed it. Then she waited, her heart beating too fast for her chest to contain it, her clothing torn, sweat coating her body—that must have made her slippery enough to escape. Still half-blind, her ears still ringing, she waited until her nose told her something was approaching, something rancid, not the clean sweet hay scent of Mustang, and swung her make-shift weapon with all of her strength and desperation.

It connected, hard enough to shed shockwaves back through her arms, rattling her teeth, and the creature went down, dropping to the ground in front of her, putting them at equal height. She couldn't look at it, couldn't bear to see its face, to see if its eyes were human, its awareness human. It needed to die, or she would die, and Maggie...

She didn't have enough strength to pull back and swing again, but, following some instinct, remembering Mustang's fight with the monsters before, she turned the chair leg around in her hands and drove the splintered end deep into the monster's flesh.

The flesh resisted, then the makeshift weapon went in with a wet, sucking noise, and she leaned on it as much as she could to force it deeper.

The body struggled, then went limp and collapsed to the floor. Elizabeth wiped the blood and sweat from her eyes even as she was scooting backward toward where she thought the sofa, and some kind of safety, was. Mustang was standing in the middle of what had once been an office, the expensive desk broken in two by the blow of his hooves, the body of the cat-monster trampled against the floor, blood staining the once cream-colored rug and bits...

She looked away, looked up. Mustang's horn was stained red, long splatters of...something thrown against his coat, his mane tangled and knotted. There was a wild look in his eye as he struck his hoof against the floor, his broad chest heaving and coated with sweat, but still ready for more, if need be. Ray was backed up against the wall, his weapon shattered on the ground, the remaining monster standing between the two of them, looking back and forth as though trying to decide which meal to eat first.

The busted doorway was empty. Elizabeth could only pray that Maggie had gotten away. She tried to stand up, and collapsed. She looked down, and realized, with an odd calm, that there was an open gash on her thigh that she hadn't even noticed, jagged and bloody and disgusting-looking.

Blood loss. That was why she was dizzy. That and being knocked around the head and thrown to the ground…. If all she had was a concussion, she'd consider herself lucky.

The thought almost made her laugh. If she died, so long as Maggie got away she'd consider herself lucky.

"Josh," she whispered, and hated herself for distracting his attention. His skin quivered, the way it did when she touched him, but he didn't take his attention off either enemy.

"Ah. Elizabeth, I had not expected hypocrisy from you, of all people," Ray said, somehow recovering his smooth bravado, although he never took his attention off the two creatures in front of him. "You railed against my beasts, and here you had one of your own. And it has two distinct forms—a were-unicorn? How wonderful. I'm sure the autopsy will give me oh, so many ideas for how to perfect the next generation."

"Over his dead body," Elizabeth said grimly, even as Mustang, ignoring the last monster, cleared the debris off the desk in one last surge, and drove his horn hard into Ray's chest.

The remaining animal howled, less angry than triumphant, and lunged for Mustang. Elizabeth would swear, for the rest of her life, that it had thrown itself deliberately onto the backward-kicking leg, taking the brunt of the blow to its thick neck. There was a crack, and it collapsed heavily onto the destroyed desk.

And the room was still.

"Oh, God. Oh, God, oh, God."

At first, Elizabeth thought the voice was hers. Then she opened her eyes, and realized that it was Maggie. Her long dark hair was pulling out of its braids, giving her sister a crazed bag-lady appearance, her eyes were wide and worried and she kept saying that over and over again. "Oh, God. Oh, God. Oh, God."

"Mags. Baby. Shut *up*."

Her sister blinked, and then started to cry. "You're alive."

Elizabeth considered that statement cautiously. "Yeah." She was a little surprised by that, but she was definitely still alive. Then her memory of the events just past flooded her, and she panicked. "Josh? Where's Josh?"

Maggie's tears were still flowing, and she made a snuffling noise, trying to keep her nose from running. "He's over there. I came in and you were both on the ground, and there was so much blood…."

Elizabeth forced her body to move, ignoring the shrieking pain in her head, and the stiffness in the rest of her body. The gash in her thigh was still bleeding and painful, but with Maggie's help, she moved slowly across the room to where Josh lay crumpled, in human form. She settled beside him, wondering if he had shifted before he passed out, or after.

"He's breathing," Maggie said. Elizabeth already knew that, even before she placed her finger at his neck to find a pulse. His chest was barely rising, but she could feel his heart pumping blood as surely as her own. Her body knew that he was alive, but oh, so hurt. Like her, his clothing was torn and bloodied, but his face was unmarked, save for a bruise in the center of his forehead where, in his other self, his horn would be.

"Josh." She called to him, her heart squeezing in anxiety when he didn't respond. "Josh!"

His eyes opened, and those dark brown eyes looked straight up and into her own. He smiled, a soft, tender, hey-there smile.

And then his entire body spasmed, his upper body bucking up off the floor, and blood began to run from his mouth and nose.

Maggie screamed, and Elizabeth grabbed at him, holding his shoulders down. What was wrong? Was he injured somewhere they couldn't see? Was it… Was it the rut he had told her about? Was this the change he had been so afraid of, about to trap him forever in his four-legged form?

The thought made her furious. No. Not now. Not after everything they had been through, after everything he had done for them! She wanted to panic but something whispered to her, giving her something to focus on.

When I'm with you...it's less painful.

Her presence made things better. Their connection soothed him. Trusting that memory, and her instinct, she leaned down and kissed him, letting the blood leave its salty tang on her tongue, mixing with her own sweat and blood, deepening the kiss until his thrashing slowed, and his breathing returned to a slow, regular rate.

She put everything she had, everything she felt, into that kiss. All her fear, her hope, her passion—her life. Letting him know that, no matter what, he would never be alone, not for as long as both of them lived.

And he had damned well better *live*.

For a terrible instant, she was afraid that it hadn't been enough. Then his hand moved, turning palm-up, fingers curling in invitation, and she covered it with her own, twining their fingers together in a promise that she was there, that she would always be there.

"M'Lizabeth." His voice was slurred, and his eyes remained closed, but the smile curving his lips was steady.

"My hero," she said, resting her forehead against his shoulder, not able right then to look at him, or to even think about the disaster that surrounded them. He was beat all to hell and back, her leg was a disaster, Maggie had a broken wrist....

And they were the ones who had won. They weren't dead. They were free.

She could feel Maggie huddled at her side, and knew that they had to get up, leave, before someone came and found them, and asked questions they could not answer. But for now it was enough to hear their heartbeats, and feel life in her veins, and know that it was over.

Chapter 15

As though their roles were reversed, Maggie fussed over Elizabeth's leg, finding a box of bandages in the shattered remains of Ray's desk and carefully binding the gash so that the bleeding, at least, would stop.

"You need to get that sewn up."

"I know." The thought of moving was almost too much for Elizabeth to bear, but too much time had already passed while Maggie sat by their sides and waited for them to wake up.

The fact that nobody had come down—the fact that nobody seemed to even know this place existed, or that the creatures lived here—suggested that the basement lab was soundproofed, but eventually one of the people who worked at those desks outside would return, or one of the bodyguards would come back, and they were in no shape to fight their way out again…and Elizabeth did not want to have to explain how Ray died. Even if they were believed, without betraying Josh's nature, they would have to deal with the discovery of the bodies of the monsters, and…no.

Eventually, someone would come down here, and then either cover it all up, or expose Ray's little Plan of Horrors. Without Ray to spearhead his terrible project, with people released from his cajoling evil, the Community could return to what it had been—a gentle, good place. Elizabeth was glad for that, glad they were able to stop any more damage from being done. But this wasn't a place for her any longer, not with the memories that would haunt her, haunt them both, the rest of their lives.

She had other concerns.

Elizabeth tested her bandaged leg, and gave Maggie a smile. "Good job, baby. Come on, help me get our guy back on his feet." The two of them helped Josh sit up. He was alert now, but still in obvious pain. "Time to get moving," Elizabeth told him. "You need medical attention, I don't care how fast you heal." She felt another wave of nausea sweep through her, and blinked. "And so do I, for that matter." Let Josh be all stoic and studly—she hurt, damn it, and wanted a doctor to make sure nothing was permanent. She saw the gun lying on the floor, and motioned to Maggie to pick it up and give it to her. They left nothing behind that could be traced back to them—or, God forbid, Kit and Lou.

"How are we going to get out?" Maggie asked, as they limped out of the shambles of the office, stepping gingerly over the motionless, furred bodies. "We can't just walk through the main hall, people will see, and they'll ask questions, and…"

Maggie was right.

"They had to get the beasts out somehow," Josh said, his voice still slightly slurred. "Not like me, can't pass. Have to have a second exit, outside of building, somewhere isolated."

"Where?" They looked around the main room; it was large, but other than the cell doors, there was no obvious exit. Six of the seven doors were open, the other still closed, its lock-pads green-lit.

"Do you think…there are still monsters in there?" Maggie asked, her voice thin again with worry.

"Don't know, don't care," Elizabeth said, but even as she spoke, Josh's body shifted forward, as though he were trying to head that way.

"Not a chance," she said fiercely, pulling him back. "If there is something in there, what are we going to do? Leave it locked up, let them deal with it!" She should feel guilty, not cleaning up the entire mess, but she didn't. Not while Maggie and Josh needed her more.

"If there's an exit, it's going to be close to the cells," he said. She took some comfort in the fact that his voice was clearer, his words better defined, and let him move forward again, still keeping a grip on his arm in case he needed help. Although, she admitted to herself, the assistance might be more from him to her...despite the wound being bandaged, her dizziness was getting worse, and she didn't have accelerated Mustang healing.

They bypassed the locked door, although Josh tried to peer into the window as they went passed, and moved into the nearest open door. The cell was about the size of a normal bedroom, with a wooden bed made up with pillows and a blanket, and an overstuffed—and shredded—chair in one corner. One wall was covered with what looked like a sisal mat, and Elizabeth realized with a shudder that one of the cat-things must have lived here—that was its scratching post. The air in the room smelled both musty and clean the way a hospital would, heavy on antiseptics and body fluids.

"They spent their entire lives in here," Maggie said, and her voice was sorrowful now. "Poor things. I wish..."

"You didn't know," she told her sister. "And even if you had, there was nothing you could do. Not unless you wanted to become part of this damned experiment, too."

What Ray had said, that Maggie *had been* part of the experiment, that they all had, stayed with her. Her parents... No, they hadn't known, hadn't ever said anything. But her grandfather had known. Would he have protected Maggie? Or would he have...

No. Her grandfather had been a good man. No matter what he had originally intended, he would never have approved of Ray's plans, would never have allowed this to happen.

It didn't matter. This place was nothing but bad memories and danger, still. The sooner they were gone from here, the better. For all three of them.

"There isn't any other door or exit in here," Josh said. "Damn it. I was sure…"

"They wouldn't want to come in here to open the door…." Elizabeth was thinking it through, being think-it-through Libby again, but it was difficult, her head fuzzy and her center of balance off. "And they couldn't risk leaving them alone with a possible exit. Whatever they had become, they were human, too, and no matter how badly they'd been twisted, once the door opened a few times they'd remember that, and use it—or try to, anyway. So…outside, but near?"

The exit they were looking for was at the far end of the row of doors, set into the wall, and accessible by the simple means of placing their hand into a shaped depression. The beasts, with their misshapen claws and padded hands, could never have managed it. The door slid open, leading them into a large stone tunnel that curved upward. Elizabeth sighed, and Maggie slid between the two of them, offering her strong, unbloodied shoulders for support. Together, ten minutes of a limping, staggering walk left them standing in a small garden on the outskirts of town, behind the maintenance shed.

Elizabeth and Josh leaned against nearby trees,

afraid to let themselves sit down, for fear they would not be able to get up again, while Maggie slid the faux-stone door back into place, to make sure nobody stumbled on the tunnel accidentally.

"Come on," Elizabeth said, looking up at the sky to try and gauge how much time had passed. "We still have to circle around to get back to the truck, and it's going to take us a while."

"I can shift—" Josh offered, and both Maggie and Elizabeth turned on him, their "no" a vehement chorus.

"We'll make it," Elizabeth said, offering him her hand. "Together."

The truck was where they had left it, untouched. By then, Josh was only limping slightly, although his cuts and bruises were still worrying-looking. Elizabeth caught a glimpse of herself in the side-view mirror, and winced. It looked like she had a nice black eye forming, and the claw marks on the side of her face were already red and inflamed.

"You're going to need tetanus shots," her sister said, not without sympathy.

"We all are," Elizabeth said. "Just to be on the safe side. And maybe rabies testing, too. Unless your people are immune to it, Josh?"

He looked up as though he was going to say something witty, then his face scrunched up and he bent over, grabbing at the door handle.

"Josh!" She made her way around the truck, cursing at her own injuries that slowed her down. "Josh, are you all right?"

"Hold me," he said. "Just…hold my hand. It needs to know you're here, that you're still here."

"Always," she said, and took his hand up in both of hers, lifting it to her mouth for a gentle kiss. As simply as that, it seemed that the pain subsided.

"You're okay?"

"I think so. But…" The spasm hit again, and sweat formed on his forehead, rolling down the side of his face as he tried to resist.

"Maggie, you drive," Elizabeth ordered, slamming open the truck's door and loading him into the cab, and then climbing in after him. She kept her hand in his, wrapping the other around his shoulders, cradling him the way she used to when Maggie had a bad dream.

"I've never driven before!" Maggie protested, but climbed in anyway, finding the keys where Josh had left them in the ignition.

"It's an automatic, it's easy," Elizabeth said. "Just get out into the road, head south and go slow."

Maggie didn't hit anything, drive off the road or attract the attention of any policemen. Other than that, Elizabeth couldn't have said anything at all about the trip back to Kit and Lou's farm. Her entire focus was on the man shivering in her arms. Josh's skin was completely filmed with sweat now, and his teeth were chattering, but his skin was hot to the touch, and every now and again it would ripple, as though he was being shaken from inside.

He was fighting off the shift, she knew. He was terrified that if he let it take over, let the rut win, he would be trapped there forever.

Guilt racked her; that he had been put to this because of her, because he stayed to make sure they were safe. He had put his entire herd in danger, if Ray discovered him, and placed his own future at risk...for them.

"We weren't worth it," she said, not even aware that she spoke.

"Yes. You are," he responded, a hoarse, hot whisper. "And that bastard...needed to be put down."

"Libby?"

Elizabeth looked up, to see that they had come to a crossroads. "When I left, Ray's men picked me up really fast after I left the farm, so I don't know which way to go...."

"Left. It's just a few miles that way."

When they pulled into the long driveway to the side of the farmhouse, Kit was waiting there. His face was stern, but not angry, and the moment they tumbled out of the truck's cab, it changed to a concerned worry.

"Lou! My bag!"

And then he was at their side, and his rough, annoyed voice was the most beautiful thing Elizabeth had ever heard. "You three, more trouble than a litter of orphaned pups. What did you do, go wrasslin' with bears this time?"

Elizabeth almost laughed, a hiccupping noise escaping her. "Sort of. We're going to need tetanus shots? I think my cuts might be infected."

The next thing Elizabeth knew, she was in an overstuffed armchair older than she was, a homemade quilt over her shoulders and painkillers in her system, her feet up on a hassock while Kit looked at her leg, cleaning it out carefully. "Not too bad," he said finally. "I'll put a liquid adhesive on it, to make sure the edges heal cleanly, but it was more bloody than anything else. Looked scary, huh?"

"Not even close to the scariest thing," she said, and Kit nodded, like he understood. Maybe he did.

Across the room, Lou was fussing over Josh, distracting him with doughnuts and iced tea, while Maggie teased the kittens with the end of her braid. Elizabeth looked at the cozy scene, and a cold hard knot in her body slowly started to dissolve.

Ray was dead. Maggie was safe. This couple—utter strangers—had taken them in and helped them, and not had a thought other than to be good neighbors. If need be, she could leave Maggie with them, while she took Josh back to his people. Maybe they could talk some sense into him, find him his virgin.

The thought sent a pang through her that had nothing to do with her bruises. The idea of letting him go, of giving him up to another woman…it hurt worse than anything the beasts had done. It hurt like losing their parents, like the fear of Maggie being hurt; a gut-wrenching, physical pain.

She would do it. To save him, she would do it. But first…she wanted a memory to hold on to.

Her leg still ached under the bandage, despite the painkillers, and her face was stiff from the salve Lou had rubbed into the scratches, with the promise that in a few weeks they wouldn't even leave a scar. Elizabeth suspected they would, that there would always be a mark from that fight. Right then, she wasn't worried about it. Maggie was tucked up in bed, under strict instructions to sleep until morning, and Kit and Lou were sitting on the front porch, talking quietly, a pitcher of iced tea on the table and the dog snoozing at Lou's feet.

No harm would come to this house tonight. There was no threat lurking outside.

Her feet carried her softly down the hall to the bedroom where Josh was sleeping. Except he wasn't sleeping. She stopped in the doorway, and her breath caught in her throat. He was sitting on the edge of the bed, shirtless, the light from the lamp casting his pale skin and blond hair into shadows.

"Josh." Was that her voice? Low and almost sultry, carrying barely across the room. He heard her, though; she suspected that he had heard her coming down the hall.

"Elizabeth. You should be…" He stood up even as he was talking, and met her halfway across the room.

Whatever objection he might have planned to make, whatever rational comment or excuse he was going to make, was lost as their mouths met, hungry and restless. His skin under her palms was smooth and hot, not feverish the way it had been before, but flame to her kindling, igniting the passion she had kept controlled all this time, hidden under fear and worry and exhaustion.

This was not a start but a farewell; she had to let him go find a virgin, a proper mate, to keep him whole and healthy.

"Will you love me, Elizabeth? Could you…for whatever time I have left?"

The question infuriated her. She wanted to yell at him, to rail at him not to be an idiot…but there would be enough time for that in the morning.

"I will be there for you, for as long as you need me," she told him instead. "In any form."

The answer didn't seem to satisfy him, but he let her lead him back to the bed, and then sat down and reached up to unbutton the long-sleeved shirt Lou had loaned her, after seeing the ripped remains of her sweatshirt. Elizabeth shivered as he exposed her skin, then again when he rested his fingers on the swell of her breasts, trailing calloused fingertips down into the plain cotton cups of her bra, grazing her nipples and making them tighten with anticipation.

"How can such a strong woman have such soft skin," he asked, before leaning forward to taste that skin for himself. Elizabeth shivered, wanting to rush him; as much as she loved the slow tender feel of his hands and mouth on her skin, she itched to return the favor; her hands stroked his bare shoulders, feeling the ripple of muscle underneath, remembering the feel of his other form under her hands and legs, as well. They had never had sex before, but they had moved together before, and she knew how to ride him…literally. The thought made her laugh, the sound as light and freeing as sound that had escaped her in what felt like…probably had been more than a year.

In that instant, she thought she could feel the weight of her parents' deaths fade. Not gone, never forgotten… but she and Maggie had a future now. And, for this night at least, that future included this man.

With that thought, she leaned forward, her hands on his shoulder pushing him back onto the bed, his feet still on the floor. She straddled him, her injured leg forgotten, her knees bent outside his thighs, and let her palms rest above his shoulders. Her body arched so that she was just over him, within reach but not touching.

"Elizabeth…" His voice was barely a whisper, his eyes dark and hooded as he gazed up at her. His hands lifted to rest at her waist, the warm fingers spanning her hips, but not pulling or tugging, just resting there, barely above the waistband of her jeans. "Your leg, and you have a concussion, you…"

"I'm fine." Any dizziness she felt was because of his nearness, the tease of his touch, his scent. She smiled down at him, and let her mouth brush across his face, a soft butterfly caress. "I want this."

The next thing she knew, she was the one on her back, his long fingers no longer resting, but working to undo the snap of her jeans, sliding them down off her long legs, careful of the area where she had been injured. Elizabeth was thankful she'd never put her sneakers back on, because she didn't think he could have managed them, he was moving so quickly.

And then he was back over her, having also rid himself of his own jeans in the process, and her breath caught in her throat. Not quite hung like a stallion, no, but she was just as thankful for that—what he brought with him in this form was more than pleasing. She shifted, reaching up to touch him, cupping the weight, feeling the texture, at once soft and scratchy against her palm, the silkiness of the shaft as she slid her hand up, slowly. He shivered, his entire frame braced against her investigation, and she could feel the impatience coursing through him.

"I want this," she said again, letting her other hand tangle in his blond mane, bringing him closer to her own body. She had said it with her kiss, but she needed the words, too, now. "I want you. Whatever form you're in. Your courage, and your kindness, and your hard-nosed attitude, and your awful sense of humor, and…"

Anything else she might have said was cut off by his mouth covering her own, then moving just as swiftly down her neck, his tongue tracing a line along her pulse even as his hands lifted her hips up off the bed. Her head pushed back into the pillow in anticipation as his mouth reached her hip bones, and his warm breath touched the delicate flesh below. The urge to be more active warred with the desire to let him take over, and only the thought that this might be their only time, their last time together, allowed her to relax into his ministrations, letting his hands and mouth explore her. His low laugh at discovering how wet she already was made her smile in response, even as a blush stained her cheeks. He shifted, allowing himself a better angle, and her smile turned into a gasp as his tongue mimicked the sexual act, diving into her slick channel then retreating, then returning again. The ache in her thighs grew, along with a quiver in her lower belly.

"Damn it, Josh…." She wasn't sure if that was a plea or a curse, but his rumble of laugher sent shock waves through her lower body, and she gave up all pretense of patience, reaching down and hauling him back up so that they were face-to-face.

The taste of her own juice in his mouth was odd but not unpleasant, and the feel of his hands gathering her up, the feel of the skin of his back and buttocks under her hand, overwhelmed everything else. She shifted, feeling the length of his shaft brush against her belly, and reached down, her hand meeting his own.

The feel of both their hands guiding him into her was the most erotic thing she had ever felt.

"Elizabeth…my Elizabeth. Mine."

His voice, rough and strained, was asking, not demanding, and she answered the only way she could, by lifting her body and accepting him inside, until their bodies were skin-to-skin, her hands cupping his backside, his bracing himself against the bed. They waited there for a second, taking in the sensation, and then, with a wicked grin, Elizabeth pushed forward against him, and he took the hint, starting them on a slow rocking motion. Skin-to-skin, their breath mingling as they moved, it felt to Elizabeth less like the first time than the hundredth or more, and yet every sensation was brand-new, sending her pulse racing and making her skin tingle with anticipation, even as the age-old motion brought her farther and farther up the familiar spiral.

What was less familiar, though, was the feeling of an echo in the sensations, as though she were hearing her own heartbeat, or…

A particularly intense shiver ran through her, but it seemed unconnected to her own rising orgasm, and in that instant she realized where it came from.

Josh.

Her eyes flew open—she hadn't been aware of closing them—and met his gaze. His normally dark eyes were all pupil, the whites almost silvery, and his skin had the same kind of hazy glow around it that she saw when he shifted.

But his body was firm and solidly human above her, inside her; the soft words he was muttering under his breath clearly understandable as curses, said so softly as to become endearments, and the look in his eyes was totally focused on her.

"I can feel you," she said. "I can feel…" Her breath caught as he pulled her forward during a surge, lifting her off the bed, bringing her forward so that she was upright, straddling his hips, face-to-face, and that change in position, that final surge, was enough to break the rising spiral and drop her into the hot, hard fall. Her body clenched around him, feeling—impossibly—the echoes of his own orgasm as a storm within a storm, each of them locked in their own private fall but shared, as well.

They collapsed onto the bed, Josh turning as they fell so that she landed half on top of him, half on her side. Sweaty flesh touched, and they were too tired, too limp with pleasure, to even think of moving away.

Elizabeth was pretty sure that the room was spinning. "That…that was…" She paused, and managed to lift a hand far enough to brush a lock of hair away from his face. "What the hell was that?"

"I…don't know." He grinned at her, a look so full of ego that she almost laughed. Then the grin faded, as though he was suddenly able to think again. "You felt me."

"Yeah."

He lifted his hand to capture her own, holding it against his chest. "I felt you. Back in the lab, I felt you. And again, here at the end, like an undertow, knocking me down, until I couldn't tell what was up or down, what was me or you…."

He stopped, and she could tell that he was doing some sort of mental inventory.

"The rut. It's gone."

"What?"

"It's gone. It's been a part of me for almost a month, Elizabeth. And now it's gone, like...like a broken bone that's finally healed, or..."

"But...how? I'm not..." She couldn't say it, even now. She wasn't a virgin, hadn't been a virgin. Hadn't been what he needed, to save himself.

Josh began to laugh, his free arm hugging her to him so roughly she let out a squeak, unable to breathe. "Because we're hidebound traditionalists, ten generations' worth," he said into her hair. "And I was so caught up in the itch, so sure what I was supposed to be looking for, my brain was totally overwhelmed by my littler, stupider head, and refused to listen to what it should have followed all along—my heart."

She shook her head, not sure what he was babbling about.

"Elizabeth, my Elizabeth. Never trust traditions. At a guess, someone translated 'untouched' to mean physically, 'pure' to mean virginal.... How could they expect you, incredible you, who stood up to monsters in human form, and faced down real monsters, who gave up everything she knew and loved to keep her sister safe, who saw a human heart inside the shape of an animal..." He let her go and shifted far enough away that he could lift her chin with one hand. His eyes were wet—so were hers. "How could they imagine anyone more untouched by evil, more pure in her love…anyone better suited to capture a unicorn?"

She shook her head, disbelieving, but a tiny shift inside her told her that it was true. She hadn't imagined it, not then, not during the battle, when she could hear his heartbeat.

She hadn't endangered him. He wasn't at risk. He had saved her…and she had saved him, in turn.

Epilogue

It was a beautiful day. The sky overhead was a pale blue, and the air was fresh and filled with the scent of grass and a healthy tang of sweat. Only some of that sweat was due to exertion.

Elizabeth was terrified. "I'm not so sure about this."

"Love, relax. You'll do fine."

"Easy for you to say. What if I smell wrong? Or say something wrong? Or…"

Josh laughed. "Impossible. You're my mate. More, you're lead mare of your own herd. We all give way before you and tremble to hear your decision."

She snorted, a noise remarkably similar to the noise made by their companions, two Mustang mares. Josh's sisters, Roseanna and Judith, were both gangly, giggling teenagers in their human form, but tall and lovely mares when they shifted. Maggie, on Judith's back, leaned forward against her sister-to-be's neck, their silent communication evident even without Maggie's particular gifts. In the two days since they had arrived at Josh's family home, the three girls had formed a tight triangle, and as much as Elizabeth missed being her sister's first confidante, she was delighted to see how easily Maggie had adapted to this new life. Maggie didn't have to hide what she could do, here.

But that made the thought of losing it all, of somehow screwing it up, all the more terrifying.

There was nothing to go back to. That life was part of the past. This was her future...maybe.

"What if..." Elizabeth ran out of questions to ask, and took a deep breath. "All right. Wait..." She waved a hand downward. "Here."

"As my lady commands," Josh said, his dark eyes sparkling, and he bowed over her hand in affectionate mockery, shimmering with the shift even as he did so. By the time she looked again, there were three Mustang standing on the hill, their coats almost blindingly white, their horns sharp and fierce, their dark eyes bright and alert. Magical...and expectant.

Her herd. If she wanted it. If she could earn it.

Elizabeth took a deep breath, and tried to soak up their love and belief in her, before turning to face the valley, and what she needed to do.

A small herd of wild horses grazed in the valley,

overseen by a single Mustang. Her white coat was shading to gray with age, but her eyes were still alert as Elizabeth approached her; evaluating the human interloper.

Grace. The herd's lead mare.

It's like meeting the in-laws for the first time after the wedding's already over, she had said to Josh that morning, when she learned what was required.

My mother already adores you, he'd said. She could tell he was trying not to laugh, but she didn't mind. He had laughed so little when she first met him, it was a revelation to hear his chuckle, spreading out like the ripples in a lake. The face that had seemed so stern, so fierce, relaxed now that they were back among his herd, and she loved to wake every morning and watch him sleep, peaceful and secure.

The same way she felt; the way she thought she would never find again. Secure…and loved.

And this one meeting could rip that all from them. If the lead mare did not accept her…

What happens then? she had asked that morning, unable to control her nerves. Josh had kissed her, so soundly that they had both forgotten everything except the touch, the scent of each other, and then touched his forehead to hers, in a gesture she now knew was how the herd greeted each other, horn against horn to show no threat, only trust.

She will accept you, he had said.

By the time she reached the bottom of the valley, the horses had wheeled and turned, coming closer. There were maybe thirty, some of them spotted white and black, others gray, and more a seemingly endless wave of brown. And one single spot of grayish-white, the dark eyes and pearly horn filling Elizabeth's gaze.

"Greetings, grandmother," she said when the mare trotted to a half a few feet away. She thought about bowing, to show respect, then decided against it. If she was to be her family's lead mare, she had to meet this woman on equal footing. Hooving?

The older mare considered her, and Elizabeth waited, holding her breath. If Grace changed to human form, was that good? Or bad? If she trotted away, what would Elizabeth do? If…

The Mustang paced forward slowly, each step the graceful movement of a four-legged waltz, never taking her eyes from the intruding human, and then turned slightly.

It took Elizabeth a moment to realize that, far from challenging her, or turning away from her, the mare was offering her side—inviting her to mount.

By now, taking the handful of mane and swinging her leg over was practically second nature, although it felt odd doing it to another Mustang; the mare was a good six inches shorter than Josh, which threw Elizabeth's movements off. She managed to seat herself easily once that adjustment was made, however. The moment the mare felt Elizabeth settle, she was off—not at a gentle walk, or a graceful trot, but a full-out run. The wild horses scattered before her, and they thundered across the grassy plains, Elizabeth's legs wrapped around the mare's belly and her hands fisted in the silky-coarse mane. After the initial shock and terror ebbed, Elizabeth was able to relax a little, secure in the knowledge that the Mustang would not step in a gopher hole or bolt at some sudden distraction. The rhythm of the mare's stride slowly soaked into her, and she adjusted her body to fit it almost unconsciously. Her elbows softened, her shoulders relaxed, and suddenly it was as though she had been born on horseback—even more so than riding with Josh, oddly enough. This was not the almost erotic melding she had with her mate, but the joyous sharing of sisters.

Elizabeth felt the wind tangle her hair, blowing the still startlingly short strands in her face, but rather than panic because she couldn't see where she was going, she merely laughed, sitting upright and letting her fingers untangle from the mare's mane, lifting her arms into the air as though to catch a handful of the blue sky.

Blue sky. The blue sky of her dreams, the smell of warm grass and clean flesh. Elizabeth laughed again, the sound rising up from deep within her.

The moment she did so, the mare's muscles shifted, and her pace slowed, until they were moving at a smooth gait barely faster than a fast walk, and then they were turning, heading back to where the wild horses had regathered, skirting them and heading up the hill to where the other Mustang, and Maggie, waited. By the time they reached the top of the hill, the mare had slowed to a deliberate walk, and Elizabeth, heeding some inner prompt, slid from her back to walk alongside her.

There was the shimmer that foretold a shift, and the mare's Mustang form was replaced with an elegant woman, old enough that Elizabeth felt a start of shame at having ridden her so hard. Then the woman turned and smiled, as though hearing Elizabeth's thoughts, and she changed her initial impression; the woman might be a grandmother, but she was strong as an oak tree, and didn't seem at all winded by their run.

"Grandmother," Josh said, taking the woman's hand in his own and kissing the age-spotted fingertips.

"We are glad to have you home, Joshua," Grace said, her voice rough and sweet as honey. "And this must be Maggie." Maggie slid down from Judith's back, and the woman looked Elizabeth's sister up and down, and then smiled. "Welcome home, my dear."

Elizabeth looked up and met Josh's gaze, the feeling still swirling within her. For a moment she saw the overlay of the Mustang, fierce and powerful, and then it faded, and he was her Josh again.

"Home," he mouthed to her silently, and she smiled, reaching out to take his free hand.

Finally. Home.

* * * * *

#145 FOREVER WEREWOLF & MOON KISSED
Michele Hauf

Forever Werewolf: While on a search for a new pack, an avalanche traps Trystan Hawkes in a castle. But when he discovers one of its inhabitants is a werewolf princess, the predicament may in fact be a stroke of luck.

Moon Kissed: Vampires destroyed his family and threaten his new love. Now a lonely werewolf, Severo, will be forced to accept a vampire into his heart if he wishes to keep the happiness he'd never thought possible.

#146 THE WOLF PRINCESS & ONE EYE OPEN
The Pack
Karen Whiddon

The Wolf Princess: Can a royal shape-shifting princess and an American doctor find love amid a palace full of dangerous intrigue?

One Eye Open: An embittered DEA agent on a hunt for the man who murdered his family joins forces with a shape-shifter searching for her brother...who just might be the killer.

You can find more information on upcoming Harlequin® titles, free excerpts and more at www.HarlequinInsideRomance.com.

HNCNM0912

REQUEST YOUR FREE BOOKS!

2 FREE NOVELS FROM THE PARANORMAL ROMANCE COLLECTION PLUS 2 FREE GIFTS!

YES! Please send me 2 FREE novels from the Paranormal Romance Collection and my 2 FREE gifts (gifts are worth about $10). After receiving them, if I don't wish to receive any more books, I can return the shipping statement marked "cancel." If I don't cancel, I will receive 4 brand-new novels every month and be billed just $21.42 in the U.S. or $23.46 in Canada. That's a saving of at least 21% off the cover price of all 4 books. It's quite a bargain! Shipping and handling is just 50¢ per book in the U.S. and 75¢ per book in Canada.* I understand that accepting the 2 free books and gifts places me under no obligation to buy anything. I can always return a shipment and cancel at any time. Even if I never buy another book, the two free books and gifts are mine to keep forever.

237/337 HDN FEL2

Name _____ (PLEASE PRINT) _____

Address _____ Apt. # _____

City _____ State/Prov. _____ Zip/Postal Code _____

Signature (if under 18, a parent or guardian must sign) _____

Mail to the **Reader Service:**
IN U.S.A.: P.O. Box 1867, Buffalo, NY 14240-1867
IN CANADA: P.O. Box 609, Fort Erie, Ontario L2A 5X3

Not valid for current subscribers to the Paranormal Romance Collection or Harlequin® Nocturne™ books.

Want to try two free books from another line?
Call 1-800-873-8635 or visit www.ReaderService.com.

* Terms and prices subject to change without notice. Prices do not include applicable taxes. Sales tax applicable in N.Y. Canadian residents will be charged applicable taxes. Offer not valid in Quebec. This offer is limited to one order per household. All orders subject to credit approval. Credit or debit balances in a customer's account(s) may be offset by any other outstanding balance owed by or to the customer. Please allow 4 to 6 weeks for delivery. Offer available while quantities last.

Your Privacy—The Reader Service is committed to protecting your privacy. Our Privacy Policy is available online at www.ReaderService.com or upon request from the Reader Service.

We make a portion of our mailing list available to reputable third parties that offer products we believe may interest you. If you prefer that we not exchange your name with third parties, or if you wish to clarify or modify your communication preferences, please visit us at www.ReaderService.com/consumerschoice or write to us at Reader Service Preference Service, P.O. Box 9062, Buffalo, NY 14269. Include your complete name and address.

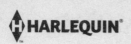

HARLEQUIN®

n●cturne™

Satisfy your paranormal cravings with two dark
and sensual new werewolf tales from
Harlequin® Nocturne™!

FOREVER WEREWOLF
by Michele Hauf

Can sexy, charismatic werewolf Trystan Hawkes win the
heart of Alpine pack princess Lexi Connors—or will dark
family secrets cost him the pack's trust...and her love?

THE WOLF PRINCESS
by Karen Whiddon

Will Dr. Braden Streib risk his life to save royal wolf shifter
Princess Alisa—even if it binds them inescapably together
in a battle against a deadly faction?

**Plus look for a reader-favorite story
included in each book!**

2 GREAT
NOVELS
SAME GREAT
PRICE

Available September 18, 2012

*Harlequin® Nocturne™ author
Michele Hauf
brings you a sneak peek of
FOREVER WEREWOLF,
a sensual new story of love and secrets colliding.*

***

Alexis Connor marched through the Wulfsiege Castle, her boots crushing broken glass, and her mind racing in twenty different directions. They'd experienced avalanches before, but never one that had been a direct hit. The medieval castle walls were thick, but she had felt the walls and floors shake, as if an earthquake had struck.

Liam raced past her with a bleeding wolf in his arms. The Irish werewolf was broad and stout, quiet yet constant. "He was just outside the doors and was slammed up against the glass when it hit," he explained to her. "His body may have been crushed but he's breathing."

"I hope Vince is all right," she said under her breath as she observed the scatter of wolves heading toward the safe sections of the castle.

Vincent Rapel was pack scion and had assumed control over the pack during the leader's sickness.

Racing to the stairs that led to the roof, where she'd be able to better assess the situation, she took them two at a time and slowly pulled open the door. A crew loitered at the edge of the roof, shovels in hand; one held a long, thin stick. A ski pole? The snow wall had pushed all the way up to the roof. As Lexi approached the men, she saw the entire court-yard had been covered over with snow. Two wolves were carefully making their way down the snow mountains formed up against the castle walls.

"What's the situation?" she asked anyone who would answer, noting that Vince was not standing in the crew. "Who is that?"

"Said his name was Trystan Hawkes," one of the men offered. "He's the one that suggested we go down with shovels and sticks to start looking for men. Just jumped right in and started work. Said time is of essence."

Lexi lifted her chin, not sure how to take that. She liked a man who took charge. Especially in a situation like this, they needed someone to take command. But did he know what he was doing?

The newcomer towered over the pack members. A natural leader who stood out among the average. He calmly delivered instructions to the men. That command appealed to her inner need for order, and touched a curious part of her that caused her to stare at the bold newcomer.

"Trystan Hawkes," she whispered against her gloved hands as she clasped them to her mouth to keep her face warm. "What have you brought to Wulfsiege?"

***

Will sexy Trystan win the heart of pack princess Lexi?

*Find out in FOREVER WEREWOLF
on September 18, 2012.*